A *Dire Wolves* MISSION

Savage Surrender

A *Dire Wolves* MISSION

ELLIS LEIGH

Kinship Press

Savage Surrender: A Dire Wolves Mission
Copyright © 2016 by Ellis Leigh

First Edition

ISBN

978-1-944336-02-8

Kinship Press
P.O. Box 221
Prospect Heights, IL 60070

To Teri Yeckl

For reminding me how much my Dire Wolves could be if I only gave them the chance. This series is because of you.

Pride is the master sin of the devil, and the
devil is the father of lies.

— EDWIN HUBBELL CHAPIN

*We have a situation. Report to the
private residence immediately.*

Bez deleted the text, pocketed his phone, and changed direction. The guards of Merriweather Fields nodded as he stalked past them. One after the other, each shifter stationed at a security point yielded without question. Bez expected nothing less. The very presence of one of his breed made even the strongest of shifters reek of fear and submission. Still, the sentries stood their ground as he passed—afraid, but not running. Terrified, but fighting their cowardice. Bez respected that. The private security staff for the president of the National Association of the Lycan Brotherhood could at least hold their posts as one of the deadliest beasts in their world passed by. Not that they knew exactly *what* he was.

Bez growled low and deep as he passed two more guards. Neither made more than a brief impression on the tracker. Still, his wolf side cataloged their features and scents. Noting any detail that made them stand out from the next. The security guards could have been a study in dominant shifter genetics. Each man resembled the next: big, buff, and mean, the kind of shifter most others would roll over and submit to without a challenge. Most shifters...but not him.

His long legs eating up the carpeted hall, Bez nearly smirked at the thought of submitting to anyone, let alone one of the president's little pets. The seven members of Bez's breed respected Blaze, agreed he'd earned it, but that didn't mean they'd submit. Thankfully, Blasius understood the dynamic of the pack when he'd asked Bez's brethren to work with him. Blasius may be president of the NALB, the ruling power over all shifters in the country, but even he didn't try to demand anything of the seven. He issued orders that the team followed, not because they had to but because they respected him enough to choose to. But in the end, the other six like Bez were a separate pack, a separate breed.

The Dire Wolves. A breed among themselves, one shrouded in mystery. An elite team of soldiers, trackers, hackers, and all-around narcissistic fucks who'd spent millennia battling side by side. They were the men called upon when the best weren't good enough, when creatures of various species needed to be found quickly or put down quietly… And Bez had been called by the only man outside of his own race he'd ever come running for.

With heightened animal instincts, a larger frame and body type than your average male, and a higher level of control over both sides of their nature than everyday shifters, the seven men in Bez's pack were a unique force within the shifter community. One handpicked by the president of the NALB to aid their intersecting causes. Most shifters considered the select seven part of the Cleaners, the designation bestowed upon the cleanup crew Blasius kept at the ready to handle NALB business. But Bez's group was even more than that designation allowed. Not that the rest of the shifter population knew their secret.

"Cleaner Beelzebub. President Zenne is expecting me," Bez said once he reached the north wing of the mansion known as Merriweather Fields. The guard, the same man who'd been stationed at this post for the last three years, nodded and moved toward the locked entry point of the heavily fortified double doors, ignoring the safety procedures they both knew were required for access to the president.

Bez glared, letting his growl grow louder as he motioned toward the retinal scanner and keypad at the side of the door. "Aren't you forgetting something?"

The guard's Adam's apple bobbed as he swallowed. He kept his head down and his eyes averted, submitting to the stronger wolf. "President Blasius is waiting for you, sir."

Bez made a humming noise as the guard opened the door. Retinal scan skipped, identity of the visitor not confirmed.

"Bez." Dante, longtime mate of Blasius, met Bez at the door, his eyes flat and his face showing signs of worry. "Thank you for coming so quickly."

Bez nodded as he stepped over the threshold, cataloging every minute detail of the dark-skinned shifter. Because that's what he did...he studied the minutia. It was a skill that came in handy, one that served his job as a tracker well. He never forgot a face, a shape, or a shadow.

As soon as the latch slammed into place, Bez grunted. "Fire the guard. He's not wolf enough to be the last line of defense between the enemy and Blaze."

Dante didn't look surprised. Bez and his team of Dire Wolves had worked for the president and Dante for too many years not to understand each other. The guard at the door would be gone within the hour.

The private wing of President Blasius Zenne—known to his most trusted allies as Blaze—was a place most shifters would never see. Blaze and his mates were living, breathing targets for any shifter, man, or beast who wanted access to the power of the NALB. But Bez wasn't most shifters; he'd been welcomed into the inner sanctum often enough to recognize a new chandelier hanging in the foyer, highlighting a picture sitting on the table to the right. One depicting the three wolves who made up the most powerful triad in North America.

The two men strode down the hall at a fast pace, neither speaking. Not until Dante closed the heavy doors at the end of the entrance hall, protecting and soundproofing the living area from all those outside.

"What's the situation?" Bez asked as soon as Dante engaged the lock.

"They've taken another Omega."

Bez didn't fight back his growl as he walked faster, his boots thumping hard on the marble floor. Omegas—exceptionally rare, powerful, female wolf shifters—had been disappearing across the continent. So far, neither the NALB nor the Cleaners and Dires had made any progress discovering why or where they were being taken to. His team's frustration was at an all-time high, the lack of information making them all feel the pressure. If there was one thing the Dires respected above all else, it was the innate power of an Omega shewolf. History hinted that the Omegas were descendants of Dire Wolves. The world thought the Dire Wolves extinct, but Bez and his breed were proof that they had survived. The attack on the Omegas was as close to an attack on the pack of seven Dires as the men had ever seen, and they'd do anything necessary to hunt down the Omega kidnappers and rescue the women.

Dante led the way down a side hall and to the private office of the president where Blaze and his second mate, a female shifter named Moira, sat looking over maps and papers. Only the most powerful shifters were blessed with two mates to create a fated triad. Just another reminder of the innate strength within Blasius Zenne.

"Blaze, he's here," Dante said as they walked in. The man in question looked up, his blue eyes hard. Blaze took his job seriously, took his responsibility to his fellow wolf shifters seriously. Anyone who doubted that fact would need nothing more than to see the fury in the man's eyes at that moment to become a true believer. The loss of another Omega was not something Blaze would take lightly.

"Thank you for coming so quickly." Blaze stood with an animalistic grace, a definite tell that his wolf was close to the surface of his consciousness. Bez noted the predatory way Blaze looked over the room, the not-quite-human cock to his head. Blaze rarely lost control, which meant something about this kidnapping had truly set him off.

"You call, I show. That's how this works, sir." Bez gripped the man's forearm and gave him a single head nod, a traditional shifter greeting showing his respect for the more dominant wolf. Blaze mimicked the motion, the move one he rarely made, showing his willingness to accept Bez on equal footing.

"Yes, well, I appreciate it." Blaze motioned Bez toward the empty couch, moving to the one where Moira sat.

"Good evening, Bez," Moira said, giving him a smile. She was new to their group, only recently found at an event Blasius and Dante hosted every December to bring fated mates together.

"They've kidnapped a fourth Omega," Blaze said with a rumble to his voice. "A young one this time."

Bez sat on the edge of the seat, leaning forward. "How young?"

Blaze shook his head, obviously reining in his wolf side as his growl tore through the room.

Moira placed a hand on Blaze's thigh, calming him, before she turned to Bez, her gaze strong and direct. "She's only fifteen. We weren't even aware this pack contained an Omega. The Alpha has refused to provide census data to the NALB for the past thirty years and didn't respond to our warnings regarding the kidnappings. What we've discovered is that the pack was relatively small with only sixteen members, all living on a single commune-style property in the Texahoma area."

"'Was'?" Bez knew the woman enough to know she wasn't one to misspeak. If Moira said "was," the news of this pack wouldn't be good.

Moira blinked and pursed her lips. "They've been decimated. Only one packmember even survived the attack other than the Omega."

"We hope." Blaze gritted his teeth, a muscle twitching in his jaw. "The survivor died shortly after being discovered, but he was able to give us a few bits of information."

Dante moved across the room, grabbing a remote to turn on the flat screen TV over the fireplace. The screen brightened, showing a picture of a man. Gritty and slightly out of focus, the picture had obviously come from a long-range camera lens. More than likely the work of Dire Wolf Levi, who collected physical pictures of the shifters he met instead of mentally cataloging them as Bez did. Good thing…the man on the screen was one Bez had never met.

"Harkens Thearouguard, formerly of the Nez Perce pack in Idaho." Dante flipped through a handful of pictures, all shots of the subject. "Seventy-eight shifter-years old, approximate look of a mid-thirties human, with dark brown hair and eyes. His wolf is an Interior Alaskan, mostly black with brown tips and shading. Last documented sighting by an NALB regional officer stated Harkens stood five feet nine in human form and approximately the same from nose to tail as a wolf. He left the Nez Perce pack eight years ago and hasn't been seen by NALB officers since. The surviving packmate recognized him as one of the attackers."

"So Harkens is my target." Bez looked over the image on the screen, memorizing every dip and line of the man's face. "Anything else?"

Dante glanced at Moira, an uncomfortable expression on his face. "The Omega's packmate was close to death when found, almost completely bled dry. The shifter who spoke to him couldn't be sure if the man was completely lucid or not at the end."

Bez sat back and cocked an eyebrow, intrigued by the hesitancy in Dante's voice. "Go on."

But Dante couldn't—or wouldn't—finish his thought. Neither he nor Blaze seemed willing to express whatever they thought might have happened to the pack.

"Oh, for fuck's sake." Moira leaned forward, face filled with fury. "Dawes kept muttering something about the attackers bringing a monster with them. One that only attacked the shewolves of the pack."

"You think they've collared a werewolf?" Bez asked, raising an eyebrow at how improbable that option seemed. Werewolves couldn't be captured and trained like circus monkeys.

She sat back with a huff. "Of course. What else do you know that would terrify a shifter and only hunt the women?"

Bez cocked an eyebrow at her sass and intelligence. She'd impressed him from the moment they'd met. In a dark hallway at the last Gathering, Moira had smiled and charmed him, protecting mates she had yet to actually meet, not knowing anything about them or their relationship with the Dire. She'd thrown herself to the lions, so to speak, and proven herself with a single, selfless act. The chick was brave, and he respected brave. Though he seriously doubted her theory of a werewolf being involved in the kidnapping.

"Moira," Blaze said, his voice quiet but filled with frustration.

Bez kept his mouth shut and his eyes on the TV screen, offering the triad what little privacy he could. He hated listening to the three argue. Like the rest of his Dire Wolf brethren, he'd never found his mate and didn't expect to. Most wolf shifters didn't make it much past a hundred without finding the person the fates had designed just for them. But the Dire Wolves differed from their cousins. All seven had lived mateless for too many hundreds of years to count.

Dante moved from the back of the couch to kneel in front of Moira and Blaze. "Werewolves only feed on female shifters, my dove. They kill anything in between them and their next meal when the full moon rises. They're mindless beasts, untrainable."

Moira's eyes went soft, her shoulders relaxing. "I know, but—"

Blaze stood and stormed across the room, pouring a glass of what looked like whiskey from a decanter on the side table. Moira quickly followed him.

Bez split his attention, surreptitiously monitoring the couple while continuing to commit Harkens' face to memory. Being part of Blaze's most trusted team and Moira's first guard, Bez knew more about their relationship than most shifters ever would. He knew exactly how much Blaze feared for Moira's safety, knew the man had just as many fears regarding Dante even though he didn't show them as openly. Bez didn't understand that kind of worry, though, having never cared about someone in that way. It all seemed excessive and time-consuming.

Finally, the two mates rejoined Dante on the couch across from Bez, neither looking happy but clinging to one another nonetheless.

Blaze coughed. "I must apologize—"

"You apologize for nothing, sir." Bez nodded toward the screen, thankful to get back on task. "Any hints on current location for the subject?"

Dante shook his head. "Before the attack, he'd been spotted a handful of times with two other shifters. It was assumed that they'd created a small, feral pack of their own, though we've been unable to confirm this. Sightings have been in New Orleans and Baton Rouge, always in late February. No one's seen him in almost a year, though."

Bez snorted and rubbed a finger across his jaw as pieces of the puzzle behind Harkens fell into place in his mind. "Of course not. It's not time yet."

Blaze swung his eyes to meet Bez's, questioning. "Time for what?"

"The brothel to open." Bez stood and headed for the door, too antsy to wait any longer. Even his wolf seemed anxious, the beast whining to be let free. Craving the exhilaration of the chase. "Miss Terri's starts taking customers in March. It's the only brothel in the South that has staff catering to a shifter's unique predilections. That kind of discretion isn't cheap, though, which means our guy's been working hard through the year to pay for his mating season concubine."

"Follow the money," Moira said.

"Exactly." Bez reached the hall and paused, looking over his shoulder to the only non-Dire he'd ever taken orders from. "Return or destroy the target, sir?"

"Return." Blaze glanced at Moira, who stared back at him, confident and strong. "I don't think he's the planner for these kidnappings, but we'll need a full interrogation to be sure. Saving the child is our end goal."

Bez nodded. "Yes, sir. You know I'll take care of it."

"I do know; that's why we called you." Blaze escorted Bez down the hall and across the threshold of two massive doors that had locked them into the private quarters. The thick, soundproof doors spanned from the floor to the coffered ceiling fifteen feet above. Dark and heavy, they highlighted the woodworking ability of another of Bez's teammates. Dire Wolf Mammon had carved them after catching a guard selling information about Dante. Mammon had figured the greedy fucker was setting up a kidnapping to usurp the president using his mate as collateral, a plan he abhorred for being weak and cowardly. Once Bez had tracked the seller and the buyer, the Dire Wolves had descended as a pack to eliminate the threat, something they rarely had the pleasure of doing. Due to the constant threat against Blaze, and the varying skills of each Dire, they tended to work apart, relying on the actual Cleaners as soldiers and backup. But on that night, they'd worked as a unit, victorious as always. Two days later, Mammon began the process of carving the doors. He whittled and planed the wood using the claws and teeth of the traitorous wolves right on the front lawn of Merriweather Fields, making sure every shifter on staff understood the penalty should one of them decide to go for money over loyalty.

The doors offered two levels of protection: one physical due to their solidness and weight, the other auditory. Once closed, the doors muffled every sound from those on the opposite side. Blaze had just shut the two of them off from Dante and Moira, thus making their conversation as private as possible, though a strong shifter out in the main hallway could overhear them should they try to. Bez assumed none of the guards in this house would try to, not knowing what the Cleaners would do to them if they did.

Bez stood at parade rest, waiting for his true orders, his neck stiff and his shoulders hard with tension. Some things were not meant to be discussed in front of others, something he had learned long ago. Something his president knew as well. Blaze threw a glance over Bez's shoulder and then leaned in close.

"The official mission states Harkens is wanted for questioning," Blaze whispered with far more air than voice forming the words, making Bez furrow his brow in question. Blaze's lips pursed for a moment. "Unofficially, you have my permission to do whatever it takes and use whatever you need of the NALB or my personal resources to interrogate Harkens your way. I want that Omega back here at the Fields in one piece, and I want you to bring the team of kidnappers in with her." Blaze leaned back, meeting Bez's steely gaze with one of his own. "Harkens isn't our guy and probably doesn't even know who the ringleader is, but he's close enough to know how to find someone who does."

Bez didn't misunderstand what the president was saying, but he still asked, "And Harkens' fate?"

Blaze's eyes glowed, his wolf pushing forward as he growled out, "A nonissue. Harkens is nothing more than a means to an end. Bring me my Omega and the people who are holding her."

"Understood, sir." Bez left Blaze in the hallway, heading for the doors out of the wing. His wolf was ready to run, anxious to get on with the hunt. And if Bez was being honest with himself, so was he. Blaze wanted Harkens dead; therefore, the shifter's last breaths were already numbered.

It was time to hunt.

Two

Sariel scraped her thumbnail over the floor, scratching a track into the wood. Another line, another day survived. Testing the depth of her latest mark, she ran her fingers over the gouges. She didn't even need to look to count them. Twenty-seven marks. Twenty-seven days locked in a houseboat in the middle of a swamp. Adding the week or so between when the men had come for her and when they threw her in her current cage, and she'd been gone from her home for over a month. It felt like a lifetime.

As the sounds of the night-loving creatures rose, heavy footsteps approached, their pace rushed. Sariel scrambled off the floor and into the corner. Hands shaking, she stood with her head slightly bent and her shoulders curved toward the wall. Submissive. Twenty-seven days alone with the same four men had taught her much, mostly how to pretend she respected them so they wouldn't take too much of an interest in teaching her their pack order. She may have no longer shown the marks from those first few lessons when she'd tried to escape or fight them, but she certainly hadn't forgotten.

"Yoo-hoo, dud. We've got a present for you."

Sariel bit back a whimper, terrified of what the present could be. She'd been lucky enough to be guarded by men who listened to their leader, and their leader said she was not to be touched. That hadn't stopped them from torturing her in other ways, though.

She cringed when the door flew open, revealing a tall shifter standing on the threshold.

"Honey, we're home." He snickered as he walked in with some kind of large, rolled package over his shoulder. Sariel sniffed on instinct, but her wolf senses had faded too much to get a good read on what he'd brought. Twenty-seven days was a long time to go without shifting, and while her wolf was still a strong presence in her mind, the physical attributes that had always been close at hand due to the wolf within had almost disappeared. She was practically human at this point.

The man tossed the package on the cot opposite Sariel's before he even looked her way. His eyes nearly glowed, his excitement almost something she could feel. And that terrified her even more. She cowered as he stalked closer, wishing for the millionth time to be anywhere but there. His grin widened at the sight of her pressing herself against the wall, a sick, twisted smile that made her want to throw up.

"Oh, dud. Don't worry, your time is coming."

"Please." Sariel shivered as his finger ran down the length of her arm. "I just want to go home."

"That's not in the cards for you, darlin'." He grabbed her wrist, pulling it to his lips and licking across the width. Sariel fought back a sob and pressed her shoulder harder against the wall. "I know you've been lonely, so I brought you a treat."

Sariel took a deep breath when he dropped her wrist. She hated him, hated the way he watched her and the constant touches he gave whenever he came near. Little things, hints of what he wanted, all adding up to make her sick whenever he came through the door. He hadn't taken yet, but she knew the yet was the most important part of that statement. His time was coming, and they both knew it. The sadistic bastard liked to tease her about what he'd do eventually, to keep her on edge.

With a knowing smirk, he chuckled before turning back toward the cot. He practically danced over to it, pulling at the fabric wrapped around the oblong shape with glee.

"See, we needed a replacement for you, since you're a dud and all."

Sariel's heart skipped and her gut clenched. "Oh, no."

"Oh, yes." He grinned as he yanked the last of the fabric. A small female, a child, really, rolled to the floor at his feet. She didn't move, didn't react. Sariel couldn't even tell if the girl was breathing.

"What did you do?" Sariel whispered, unable to hold back the words.

The man grinned and shrugged. "We found someone who wasn't a dud."

"No." Sariel's stomach sank and her eyes burned. This was her fault. Her stupid, defective body had been the catalyst for these animals to hunt the poor girl. She wasn't stupid—she knew the reason they called her a dud. Sariel had known it since she was a pup. She didn't have a functioning reproductive system, which her captors had discovered when they'd forced her to endure two days of invasive medical exams.

"Don't worry," he growled, his voice a shade too high not to be mocking her. "We've got a plan for you as well."

He prodded the girl with his foot before walking to the door, leaving behind the blanket he'd had her wrapped in. Sariel waited until he slammed the door before she left her corner. She stepped lightly, moved slowly and softly across the room. She almost didn't want to know if the girl was alive or not. She hoped she was, prayed even, but deep down, Sariel wondered if it would be better for the girl to be dead. Whatever those monsters had planned, it involved shewolves being used in ways that evoked her worst nightmares. And the gods forbid that fate be bestowed on a child.

"Please, oh please, oh please." Sariel dropped to her knees and crept the last few inches toward the girl, holding her breath. With her hands shaking, she reached for the girl's throat. A pulse pounded slow but strong. She was alive.

Sariel didn't know if she should be relieved or disappointed in that fact.

Three

Bez raced across the marshy ground, his claws gripping at whatever purchase they could find, his stride long and aggressive. His prey ran ahead, just out of his sight, the sounds of him slipping and sliding across the wet ground giving away his location. The animal remained just out of Bez's reach, not that Bez worried about the distance. Time had taught him many things, one being the necessity of patience when on the hunt. His body toned, his breathing measured, he dropped his head and ran harder, using his nose to guide him. The scent trail left by the animal in front of him practically glowed in the moonlight, a strong and wide light leading the way, stinking of fear and adrenaline. His prey was scared…as well it should have been.

As Bez leaped over a fallen tree, he caught sight of his quarry running through the tall grass. Dark and thin, the wolf looked too small to be a shifter, but Bez knew the truth. A man lived inside that wolf body; one Bez had been hunting for nearly three weeks. Through seedy bars and outlaw shifter communities, he'd tracked the beast before him, hunting down every clue, roughing up any witness who dared to refuse to speak. Three weeks of little rest for the hunter. It was time for the chase to come to an end.

Demanding one last burst of speed from his body, Bez lengthened his stride and pumped his legs harder, gaining on the smaller animal. Reaching, clawing, running, stretching—Bez gave himself over to his animal side, letting his wolf out to do what it did best—until the prey offered up the perfect target. Bez lunged, his teeth clamping down on the other animal's back hock. He jerked his head, flipping the smaller wolf on his back, satisfied in his conquest only when he heard the snap of breaking bones.

Once the animal lay panting in the grass, Bez crawled over the top of him. Feet on either side of the fallen wolf, Bez pulled his lips back in a snarl, ready to pin his prey if need be. The animal didn't fight back, though. Instead, he closed his eyes and whimpered, angling his head to show his neck to Bez. Submitting to the more dominant wolf. Weak bastard. Knowing he had the upper hand, Bez took a step back, keeping his eyes on his fallen prey as he shifted to his human form.

"You've given me quite the run, Harkens." Bez shook off the last of his change, a familiar chill going down his spine as fur turned to skin. "Now, get human; we need to have a talk."

The fallen wolf didn't move except to attempt to stretch out his back leg. At least that's what Bez assumed—whatever bones had broken during the capture flip had left the animal unable to do much more than twitch. Bez stared at his prey, waiting for compliance, calm in the face of the disobedience. But after a few minutes where the wolf did nothing more than shake and whine, Bez sighed. Some people simply couldn't accept defeat.

Bez leaned over the fallen animal, letting his wolf push past his human side enough to feel the warmth of the animal power in his blood. Focusing on his prey, Bez put a hand across the other animal's forehead and met his watery gaze.

"Shift, now."

The wolf's whimpers turned first to frightened growls and then to screams of pain as his human body ripped through his wolf form. Naked and shaking, the twisted man lay in the mud at Bez's feet. Thin…pale… weak.

"I'm not telling you shit," Harkens spat even as his breathing turned to pained pants.

"I don't need shit. I need to know about the missing

Omega, the young one."

Harkens groaned as he tried to roll onto his stomach, the bones in his back and shoulders not complying with the movement of his muscles. "I don't know nothing."

"Double negative." Bez put a bare foot on Harkens' ribcage.

"What the hell—" Harkens' scream cut off whatever he'd planned to ask. Not that Bez would have answered him. He was too busy forcing his foot down on Harkens' broken ribs.

"Double negative, fucker. 'Don't know nothing' means you know something. I'm giving you one chance to tell me what I need to know. You do that, I kill you nice and easy right here." Bez smiled as the man's eyes grew wide. Harkens' scent went harsh and slightly bitter, making Bez's wolf practically salivate with glee. Yeah, he liked the scent of fear on this one.

When Harkens still didn't speak, Bez nudged his foot higher, pressing harder. "You make me ask again, your death will still come, but it won't be nice or easy."

"Fuck you," Harkens spat through trembling jaws.

"Wrong answer." Bez grabbed Harkens, picking him up and slinging his broken body over his shoulders. Harkens screamed and cried, trying to wiggle out of Bez's hold, but to no avail. Bez ignored every sound, every movement, and carried his prey out of the marshlands.

When Bez reached his Jeep, he tossed his load in

the back seat. Harkens cursed and attempted to crawl out of the open-topped vehicle, but Bez had been a hunter for a long time. No one escaped him once he set his wolf upon their trail.

Keeping one hand on Harkens' ankle, Bez reached under the passenger's seat for the metal handcuffs he stashed there. He had another pair under the driver's seat and two more in the very back. Bez was nothing if not prepared, thanks in part to the mechanic of the Dire wolf pack, Luc.

As Bez fastened the cuffs to Harkens' ankles and wrists, essentially tying him to the frame of the Jeep, he clucked and shook his head. "I was trying to be nice, but you had to make things difficult. Now, we get to do things my way."

"Oh, please," the injured man huffed, still fronting as if he could somehow best Bez. "You think I'm afraid of you Feral Breed fuckers? You have no idea who I work for."

"Nope, I don't." Bez clasped the last cuff to the base of the roll bar and strode to the driver's side of the vehicle, fighting back a smile. So Harkens assumed he was a Feral Breed member? Not that he had anything against the motorcycle club Blaze used as a more localized police force. Hell, he'd even worked with some of them the previous year when the kidnappers almost managed to get their hands on another Omega. He liked the team he'd met in the Upper Peninsula of

Michigan, but the Feral Breed had nothing on a Dire Wolf.

Bez hopped into the driver's seat, not bothering with the door. "I'm not a Feral Breed member. I'm far worse than those pups."

"So, what, you're a Cleaner? Blasius so afraid of us he sent out his private guard dogs?"

Bez shrugged as he reached under his seat for a pair of jeans and a black T-shirt. "You could call me a Cleaner, or not. You're dead either way."

Harkens snorted. "Yeah, right. Give me half an hour for these bones to heal, and we'll see who's the one dying."

"You're all talk, Harkens." Bez grinned and pulled on his clothes, tossing a rough blanket over his shoulder to cover the other man's nudity. He didn't need to get pulled over on the way to the safe house because Harkens was letting his junk air out.

Harkens used his legs to push himself farther up in the seat, a sure sign his bones were healing. "You're all brawn with no brain. You think I can't get away from you?"

"Nah, man…you can't." Bez met the man's eyes in the rearview mirror, letting his wolf come forth to swirl the color around the iris the way only Dire Wolves could. "No one's ever escaped me."

"Bullshit." Harkens tried to sound strong, but his eyes were blown wide and his heart pounded loud enough for Bez to hear from his seat up front. "The only tracker the NALB had with a perfect record was Beelzebub, and he's been dead for over twenty years. Fucking vamp took care of that psychopath."

Bez grinned as he spun out on the dirt. His wolf made a stronger appearance, forcing his canines to lengthen and the corners of his eyes to pull up into their more lupine placement. Cocky fucker liked to be reminded of his last fight with a fully matured vampire, even if the story the shifter world knew was completely wrong. "So glad my reputation precedes me, but I wasn't dead. The vamp tried, though. He tried hard."

When Harkens made a strangled sound, Bez glanced in the rearview mirror again. Harkens had gone even paler, looking as if he'd seen a ghost. Which, Bez guessed, he kind of had if the man thought a vamp had taken him down.

"Holy shit, you're…"

Bez gunned the engine as he hit the highway, growling into the wind. "That's right, Harkens. You're dancing with one of the devils of the breed tonight."

Four

The retching started shortly after the sun set. Sariel was already prepared, ready with the bucket she'd been forced to urinate in and a towel. The cloth was filthy, as was everything in the nasty prison, but it was the best she could do.

"Easy, now." Sariel poured clean water from the pitcher their captors brought in every day onto the towel to dampen it, then placed it against the back of the girl's neck. "Don't fight it. You'll feel better once you've gotten rid of the drugs."

The girl cried and coughed, clutching the bucket as she emptied her stomach. The sounds, the smell, all of it reminded Sariel of her own first few days on the boat. Of the sick feeling as the drugs her captors had forced on her worked their way through her system.

The fear of not knowing where she was or who the men guarding her were. The terror at what their plans were. She remembered every second, but she'd been forced to handle it all alone. The girl at least had Sariel on her side, and she would do everything she could to protect her.

"Shhhh." Sariel ran a hand over the girl's back as the vomiting slowed. "It's awful, I know. Give it a minute and it'll stop. Then you can have a drink."

The girl choked, a sad, coughing noise coming from her as she fought back her sobs. Sariel remembered that, too. Though she'd let her tears fall those first few days. And been punished for them.

"Don't cry. I'm here, and I'll help you. Just don't cry."

The girl quieted before taking a deep breath. "Where am I?"

"Some sort of swamp. I don't really know much more than that."

The girl sniffed and raised her head, taking a look around. She had huge, dark eyes that were red-rimmed, but pretty. Sweet-faced and petite, she looked like a teenager. A thought that turned Sariel's stomach. She was just a kid.

The girl sat quiet for a few long moments, doing nothing more than breathing, it seemed. Sariel waited, watching her. Hoping she would stay calm as the reality that had been thrust upon her truly settled into place.

"Not Florida," the girl said, her voice soft but sure. "Bayou, maybe."

Sariel cocked her head, her brow tightening. "What?"

The girl shrugged and pulled her ash-colored hair away from her face. The strands caught the little bit of light pushing through the windows, practically glowing. Sariel had never seen such a color on a human before. Brown and gray and black, all woven together with streaks of silver interspersed throughout. She bet it was gorgeous when it was clean and brushed.

The girl nodded toward the window. "It doesn't smell like the Everglades, so if it's a swamp, my guess is bayou country. Louisiana, more than likely."

Sariel huffed a laugh. "Well, you're certainly smarter than I am. I couldn't have told you a thing about this place other than the air is as heavy as a wool blanket."

The girl's mouth tipped up in a tiny smile. "My mom has family outside of Miami. My brother and I spent a lot of time in and around the Everglades."

She grew quiet again, pensive, probably stuck on thoughts of the family and pack she'd been taken from. Thoughts Sariel knew too much about.

"I'm Sariel," she said, trying to draw the girl out again. To give her a sense of normalcy in this unusual situation. "I'm an only child and one of only three shifters younger than eighty in my pack. I grew up in the desert outside Yuma, Arizona."

The girl stared at her for a long moment, those dark eyes going from near lifeless to filled with a rage that took Sariel by surprise. "I'm Angelita, and I had a little brother who was my world back in Texas. But he, my parents, and my pack are dead. Those bastards who took me killed them all."

Five

Bez stood in the kitchen of the hunting cabin he'd been holed up in for the past three days, sipping coffee and looking over emails on his phone. The house was one of Blaze's property holdings. The man had little cabins to large mansions scattered across the country and beyond. All in secluded locations, all stocked to the rafters with weaponry and supplies in case he needed a place to hide, most with shifter-proof safe rooms as added protection for his mates. The president had a plan for almost anything, and the Dire Wolves were the only men on his private security team to not only have access to each property but to have the passcodes and weaponry inventory for each and every house. Something that came in handy when they were hunting down a target. Or trying to get one to talk.

A gurgle from the living room alerted Bez to the start of his workday. Another session, another fight not to kill the fucker in the other room before he got what he needed. And he would get it—he never fucking failed a mission.

Bez put his phone back in his pocket and drank down the last of his coffee. He washed out his mug in the sink, making sure to dry the heavy ceramic vessel and place it back in the exact spot where he'd found it. A second gurgle and a moan sounded as he wiped down the counters, but Bez stayed focused. He had to remove all traces of his presence in case he needed to make a quick exit. There was a precision to this job, a methodology learned over centuries of training. He would not be rushed.

Humming while he worked, Bez cleaned every inch of the kitchen until it sparkled. When he finished, he reached into a drawer and grabbed what he needed before turning toward the space most people would use for a living room. Bez had used it in a bit of a different way. Of course, his job wasn't what most people would call a job.

"You ready to talk yet?" Bez looked over at Harkens. The shifter hung midair, suspended by a chain around his ankles and secured to the ceiling. Head down, arms tied to his chest to keep from dangling, Harkens rocked slightly over the tarp Bez had spread across the hardwoods to keep the floors clean.

A job well done, but he wasn't finished yet.

Shifters were a hard breed to kill, though not as hardy as some of the monsters Bez had hunted over the years. Still, shifters had a regeneration ability that defied human logic. To kill a shifter, you needed to stop his blood from flowing. There were two ways Bez preferred to accomplish that task. The first—tearing out the heart of the aforementioned shifter—offered a quick and relatively painless death, though it wasn't really a choice if you needed information and the target refused to speak. Like Harkens.

The second way had been Bez's only option given the situation.

Bez had been bleeding the shifter slowly over the three days he'd had him suspended from the ceiling, killing him bit by bit, a handful of strategically placed slashes and artery nicks added every day. It looked like a gory and painful way to die, but that tended to make lips move. And Bez's mission was to find the Omega, not to help his informants make a peaceful transition to whatever afterlife they were due.

Harkens coughed, spraying blood across the tarp below him as he did. Bez glowered at the mess until a weak whisper reached his ears.

"Attakapas."

Bez moved closer, circling Harkens. His wolf perked up and pushed against his human mind, finally seeing an end to the wait for the real mission in sight.

"What's Attakapas?"

"Camp." Harkens coughed again, choking this time on the blood pooling in his mouth. "She was to be taken to a camp near the Attakapas Refuge. Please. Please let me down."

"How many men?" Bez waited for an answer before using his foot to swing the man around. He squatted and tilted his head, growling as his wolf wrangled for control. The beast was ready to end this...to kill the weaker animal and move on to the next hunt. But Bez still needed information. "How many men guard the Omega?"

"A handful. Spread thin. Five, maybe."

"That sounds like bullshit to me."

"The camp is in the swamp, deep in. Boss thinks no one can find it, plus he sent—" Harkens coughed again, his entire body swinging and jerking with the force.

The blood hit the wall, making Bez twitch. Harkens would be dead soon, of that he had no doubt, so cleanup would have to wait. No matter how much he hated to admit that.

"Who's this boss? What's his name?"

"Don't...know. Call him...The King."

"Someone thinks highly of themselves." Bez stood and circled his prisoner, considering his options. "So that's it? Attakapas, somewhere in a bayou that stretches over what...probably a hundred miles? Five men guarding the Omega. Anything else?"

Harkens hung quiet, eyes open but unfocused. Alive and yet…not.

"Your usefulness has ended." Bez struck fast and hard, brandishing the knife he'd been palming and slitting the other man's throat in a single swipe. What little blood was left sprayed toward the wall, but Bez ignored it. The thrill of the hunt was back, and that meant he needed to move. Without a pause, he dropped the knife and grabbed his phone, pressing a button as he walked out the front door.

"Attakapas Refuge," he said when Dante answered. "That's the holding spot—some camp in the swamp. Five guards, tops."

"Need backup?"

"Not for the initial mission; I should be able to handle that hunt alone. Alert Levi just in case, and call Mammon to put the Dires on standby for the phase-two hunt. Last I heard, he was over in Fort Worth keeping an eye on thet new pack of shifers. I want men no more than four hours away before I get back from the field."

"On it."

Bez strode across the lawn toward his Jeep, taking one last look over the property. "Also, I'll be selling the house at my current location."

"Selling?" Dante's voice carried a bristle to it that Bez didn't often hear. Though, he rarely made messes that warranted such an action. "May I ask the reason?"

"It's not clean enough."

Dante didn't answer, but the sound of clicking keys told Bez he was typing. "Tracking you now. Take care of the sale; I'll handle the residual paperwork."

"Understood." Bez ended the call and gave himself one final moment to look over the property. He always loved their version selling a house, though it wasn't something they did often. That would attract too much attention, as would a man standing in the driveway staring at a house that was about to disappear. It was time to go.

Eyes on his phone, looking up the closest property to Attakapas Refuge, Bez hopped into the Jeep. He cranked the engine while reaching for a black remote in the glove box, having already set up everything he needed to "sell" this place before he'd even walked in the door three days ago. When he reached the end of the driveway, Bez grinned and pressed the single white button on the face of the little device.

After a moment's delay, the cabin exploded, the resulting blaze hot enough to burn the inside of Bez's nose as he inhaled. He dropped the remote, grabbed his shades from the visor, and turned onto the main road. Attakapas Island Wildlife Management Area was a little over six hours away. The Omega was within grabbing distance.

Six

ariel woke from her nap suddenly, her heart racing in her chest. God, her dreams…such wistful, heartbreaking visions of the past playing out as her mind surrendered to fantasy. Pictures of home dancing through her head, the feel of hard earth under her paws, and the exhilaration that only came from running in her wolf form across the harsh yet beautiful terrain. She missed it, missed everything terribly. In her dreams, she was home in the desert, surrounded by her pack. But when she woke up… Well, that was when she fell into an entirely different reality. One that had been forced on her. One she didn't know if she could survive.

The sound of sniffling from across the room whispered in the thick, humid air, just loud enough for her sensitive ears to pick up. Angelita was crying again. The little shifter who'd been tossed into the houseboat only a week before had been doing that on and off for days, hiding her face in her pillow and sobbing, thinking no one knew. But Sariel knew… She heard the muffled cries, and she worried for the young girl. Possibly even more than she worried for herself.

The teenager had woken up terrified, screaming and crying on the floor of the houseboat not long after their guard had left. It had taken Sariel almost an hour to get the girl to calm down enough to speak. Another two to get her to tell Sariel her name. It took Angelita three days to finally admit how the men, assumedly the same ones who had whisked Sariel away in the middle of the night, had attacked her pack and killed her family. The little girl had been made an orphan and a prisoner within a matter of hours, and Sariel's heart broke every time she saw the overwhelming grief on Angelita's pretty face.

Sariel ran her hand over her eyes and sighed, somewhat frustrated. She couldn't blame Angelita for being upset, but tears did nothing but make the men around them want more. And the animals that'd kidnapped them both—that had swooped into their regular lives and dragged them away to this humid, stinky hell in the middle of a fucking swamp—would get those tears from the pup one way or another if she didn't stay quiet. They considered it a game, one they played with their captives whenever they got bored. And the bastards got bored often. Sariel had learned that quickly, and she'd make sure the young one knew it too. Buck up, don't give them anything to work with, tuck your emotions under your inner strength, and pretend to be submissive to their wolves to keep them from trying to prove their dominance. She would make sure Angelita learned how to survive this place without the harsh lessons Sariel had endured.

As another sob wrenched through Angelita, Sariel glanced at the chair by the door. Empty. She turned back toward the young shifter's cot, thankful their guard had left them alone for the moment.

"Angelita," she hissed, keeping her voice as soft as possible. "Honey, you need to calm down."

The girl went silent for a minute, trying hard to obey, but then a choked sob broke through the thick afternoon air. The sound tore at Sariel's heart, reminding her of just how young Angelita was. More so than her fifteen short years would indicate, really. The girl had been sheltered by her pack. Protected. Sariel was a mature shifter who'd seen the good and bad of life come her way, and she could barely hold herself together under the constant fear their situation blanketed her in. Poor Angelita didn't have a chance… not alone, at least.

Sariel slid out of her bed and snuck across the wood planks, praying she didn't hit a squeaky spot. The last thing she needed was to draw the attention of the men keeping them in this fetid trash dump they called a houseboat. When she reached Angelita's bed, she knelt on the rough floor and pulled the sheet back from over the girl's head. Even in the dim light the filthy windows allowed into the room, Sariel could see the puffiness of Angelita's eyes, the angry red streaks burning paths down her cheeks. This cryfest had been going on for a while.

Placing a calming hand on Angelita's shoulder, Sariel leaned over her and whispered, "If they hear you, they'll come in here. And then things will be worse."

Angelita nodded and sniffed. "I know."

"Then why are you crying?"

The girl was quiet for a minute, only the sounds of insects Sariel couldn't even identify invading the still, humid air. Thick…she'd never known air could actually feel thick. Good Lord, it was like trying to breathe through a wet blanket all the time.

"I'm scared," Angelita finally admitted. Sariel rubbed her shoulder and inched closer. Angelita's eyes opened wide, staring at her, making Sariel's chest hurt with the amount of pain she could see carried within them. Angelita was afraid, alone, and grieving… Sariel could at least try to help with two of those.

"I'm scared too, and with good reason. But tears won't do nothin' more than make you weak, and we can't afford to be weak. We have to be strong right now, little one. Stronger than those men out there."

"I'm trying. But sometimes…" The girl trailed off, looking at the ceiling. Sariel waited for her to finish her thought, rubbing a hand over her hair to try to calm the young one's nerves. The weeks spent trapped in this place had been hell on earth for Sariel, but to the girl, who'd lost her entire family and pack when the men holding them had raided her home to snatch her, it must have been pure torture. She had nothing here to cling to and nothing from where she'd been raised to go home to. That thought always made Sariel's protective instincts surge, made the motherly feelings she thought had skipped past her come roaring to the front of her mind. Everyone deserved a place to call home.

After several quiet moments, Angelita took a deep breath, her voice stronger as she said, "Sometimes I remember what they did to my mom and dad, and I can't decide if I want to hurt them or cry. So I cry, because I can't hurt them." Her eyes met Sariel's, glowing brightly, the power of her wolf pushing through her human side. "At least not yet."

"That's right," Sariel said, wishing she could let her own wolf peek out of the cage she'd been keeping her in. She'd learned the hard way not to shift in this place, not to even let her wolf senses free. If she wanted to stay alive, she'd have to do it in her human form, without the help of her greatest ally. "We'll get them back for what they did to your family."

Angelita wiped away the last of her tears, sounding small and shy as she whispered, "We'll get out of here eventually, right?"

"Yes, ma'am," Sariel said, fighting back her doubts. "There's no way I'm staying in this hellhole forever."

"But what about the alligators? That one guy said gators aren't afraid of wolves."

Sariel rolled her eyes. "Honey, I'm afraid of a lot of things. Uncontrollable male shifters, knives being thrown, tight spaces, fire ants. But I'm not afraid of some prehistoric throwback swimming around out there in that murky water. I'm from the desert; we've got nasty stinging critters and snakes galore." Sariel pointed toward the far window, the only one that opened to allow fresh air in. "But that swamp? That's our escape, our way to find a new home, our only shot at survival. That's freedom out there. And no way is some reptile getting in the way of me and freedom."

"So what do we do?"

"We listen...and we watch. Knowledge is our most powerful weapon, little one. We keep our eyes on these men and figure out what's what. Like that the dark one can't smell his own scat, or the tall blond seems to have a little hearing trouble. Stuff like that can be used to our advantage, right?"

Sariel smiled as Angelita nodded. "A little bit longer, and we'll have our chance. It's just a matter of time. Those boys out there think they have a couple of delicate petals on their hands. They've never truly seen what happens when one of us shows our claws."

Angelita was quiet for a moment, her lips pursed. "What if they come for us before then, or they split us up?"

Sariel's stomach dropped, but she held her tongue. She'd heard a conversation about just that thing the other day. They needed Angelita somewhere up north, and Sariel wasn't needed at all anymore. She'd never thought her being sterile would be a good thing, but having been kidnapped by a group who only wanted her so they could breed her had changed her mind in a hurry. Every day, she thanked the stars for that little biological defect. But Angelita wasn't as lucky. The men had left her alone so far, other than to tease and torment the child, but she knew that would end once they got her to wherever they were planning to take her. Angelita was in serious danger, and Sariel could only hope they'd be able to escape together before it all came to a head.

Doing her best to keep her face calm and clear of the worry eating her up from the inside, Sariel tucked the dirty sheet around Angelita's shoulders. "Don't go borrowing trouble, now. We have three things to do—watch, wait, and plan. If we do that, we get out. Period."

Angelita nodded, snuggling into Sariel's side. The two lay quiet and still, listening to the chorus of insects buzzing away. Frogs croaked and splashed, birds screamed, and alligators roared in the distance. Noises Sariel had somehow gotten used to. And by the gods, wasn't it a sick, sad fact that she'd been there long enough to get used to all that?

"What do you want to do when you get out of here?" Angelita asked, breaking the heavy non-silence.

"Besides shower for a whole day?" Sariel winked and smiled, the two of them both uncomfortable with their lack of bathing options. "I want food…real food. And I'd like to find myself a handsome shifter to hold on to for a few hours."

The girl giggled, reminding Sariel of how young she really was. Not just in years, but how inexperienced and immature she could be. The princess of her pack, Angelita was the epitome of a sheltered young woman. Too old to be a child, not yet ready to be a woman. Trapped in the in-between where emotions ran strong and every disappointment seemed to bring on the end of the world. Sariel hoped she could help her get out of this place, to give her the chance to grow up a bit more somewhere safe and secure. Somewhere they'd honor her and protect that innocence as they introduced her slowly to what it meant to be a woman.

But even knowing how careful she needed to be, Sariel wasn't going to lie to the girl. Not about her hopes for when they escaped. If it made Angelita blush, so be it. She'd understand the draw of big, strong arms wrapping around her one day.

"And when I'm clean," Sariel said, grinning at Angelita's blush and looking up at the ceiling. "When my belly's full and I've kicked that nice shifter back to where he came from, I want to go north."

Angelita snuggled closer, tangling their legs together for the comfort of touch. "Why north?"

But, oh, there was danger in that answer. Sariel shrugged, trying to hide the wet burning in her eyes and the way her hands shook. "I've never seen snow, and I think I might like to."

Angelita grew quiet, her face serious as she stared at Sariel in a way that made her think the young one knew why she wanted to see snow. Just once. Because the fact that she'd been kidnapped and brought out to this hellhole in the bayou had put the possibility that her life may end on the front burner in her mind. She was in trouble, and so was Angelita. If Sariel got out of this mess, she was doing all the things she'd put off before the night those men stormed into her home. She was doing all the things she'd ever wanted to so that she didn't feel as if she was missing anything. She was living the life she'd always dreamed of, whether her pack liked it or not.

Seven

The late winter sun blazed bright in the western sky as Bez pulled up outside the lake house. The place looked surprisingly well-kept considering how long it had sat empty, though there was a definite air of abandonment to the property. Not that Bez cared much for whether the house was visually pleasing—the location sat close enough to where the Omega was being hidden to use for a stronghold. That detail outweighed any other factors. Hell, Bez would have picked a hunting platform in a tree if he'd had to.

Like all of Blaze's personal properties, the lake house offered privacy, positioned far enough from any other houses to keep nosy neighbors away. A necessity when dealing with men who could turn into wolves at the drop of a hat. Perched on a slight hill and looking over one hundred yards of grass in the three directions away from the lakefront, there was no way to stage an attack on the single-story home without being seen or heard first. An easily defendable location that, if the records Bez had read about the property were still accurate, was filled with weaponry and emergency evac supplies...exactly what he needed.

He used the keypad lock by the garage to gain access to the house, satisfied with the steel fire doors. They wouldn't necessarily keep a shifter out if one wanted in, but they'd slow him down and make his entrance loud instead of stealthy. Perfect for those inside the house.

As expected, the kitchen contained numerous containers filled with non-perishable food and bottled water. Enough for three people to survive for a couple of months at least. Blaze didn't do anything halfway. Bez grabbed a bag of beef jerky and continued through the house, sniffing out every possible hiding place and peeking behind every door.

The ringing of Bez's phone interrupted his investigation, though. He snorted when he saw the name of the incoming caller.

"What's up, old man?" Bez asked, leaning against the bedroom wall and peeking out the window overlooking the lake.

Deus, one of his Dire Wolf brethren chuckled. "Fuck off, kid. At this point, the fact that you're two weeks younger than me is a nonissue."

"That's your opinion." Bez walked back out to the living and dining rooms, pacing through the two, anxious. "What's doing?"

"Why the fuck are you down in Louisiana?"

"You stalking me again?" Bez shook his head. He shouldn't have been surprised. Deus had every one of the guys outfitted with chips in their phones and cars. Mammon liked to joke that the man would have them all microchipped like some puppy next.

"Nah, just got a ping from one of Blaze's lake houses down there, and it coincided with your GPS location. Figured you were gator hunting or some shit."

Bez spun in place, looking harder at the walls and fixtures, wondering what door or motion detector had set off a notification to Deus. And how he hadn't noticed it. "Negative. Got a mission from Blaze."

"Anything you need me for?"

"Not yet. I've got a solid plan in place and some of our brothers chilling in the wings."

"All right, then. Call if you need us." Deus hung up, not giving Bez a chance to reply. The man never did stay on any one subject long, too busy with his computers to bother with people most of the time.

Determined to find the supplies he needed, Bez set back on his investigation of the house. After almost a quarter-hour of snooping through closets and behind doors, he found the cabinet filled with guns and weaponry. Shotguns and automatic rifles stood at the ready, and large metal drawers housed ammunition, handguns, and explosives. In a bottom drawer, Bez found his personal favorite. Large, flat brass rings lay on a wooden support with a dowel shooting through the center. Designed off the Indian throwing rings known as chakrams, the rings practically glowed in the light, beautiful and polished to a sheen. A very deadly sheen. Dire Thaus, the weaponry expert of the group, had taken ancient chakrams and reworked them to fit the hunting style of the Dire Wolves. Light and easy to throw, the rings fit across the width of Bez's hand. Perfectly weighted for flight. Perfectly sharpened to cut through even the thickest of enemy flesh in near silence. Perfectly designed to fit in the pocket of his black fatigues, which was right where a few of them were going. Just in case.

His phone rang again, though this time, the caller's name made Bez roll his eyes.

"What, kid?"

"Why you gotta do me like that, bro?" Levi laughed, a near-constant sound from that particular brother. "I got a buzz from Dante that I need to stick close to you for a bit. What's doing?"

"Mission. Another Omega missing."

"Motherfucker." Levi didn't laugh again, not that Bez expected him to once he knew what the mission was. The Dires were pissed as hell about the attacks on the ones they saw as their kin. Even Levi, the jokester of the group—the one who partied harder than all the rest and took advantage of all the world had to offer a six-five, muscular, good-looking kid like himself in terms of women, liquor, and adventure—raged whenever word reached him that another Omega was in trouble. They all had a soft spot for the shewolves, though Bez had a theory that Levi's soft spot was bigger than anyone else's. He seemed to take each disappearance as a personal challenge to take more risks, stroll into even more dangerous situations all in the name of finding the shewolves. Something that made the rest of the team nervous, including Bez. To accomplish their missions, they all needed to be on point, on plan, and in control of their instincts. Levi pushed every boundary they set and quite possibly endangered every mission.

"What's the plan?" Levi finally asked, his voice rough, his anger clear underneath the words. A man ready to lock and load. But Bez couldn't risk the girl to Levi's cowboy antics.

"I hunt. You stay close as assigned."

"I can come down and hunt with you. I'm not that far—could be there by tomorrow morning."

"Negative. Protocol in these situations states the initial hunt should be solo."

Levi growled loud enough for Bez's wolf to push forward. To growl back at what he saw as a challenge.

"Fuck protocol. We've got an Omega in trouble. Let me help."

Bez considered telling him the full story—about how the captors killed her pack and how she was just a child—but he didn't want to set Levi off any more than he already was. Loose cannons rarely won wars. "Stand down, Leviathan. I've got this covered. You be my shadow and keep your ass close."

Levi was quiet for longer than a pause, but Bez knew he was reining himself back in. The kid had been through just as much military training as the rest of the Dires, but he still struggled with execution on missions. Bez couldn't have that sort of unknown element with this assignment.

"Fine," Levi finally spat. "I'll be at the three-hour mark from your coordinates."

"Four."

"Three, or else I'm showing up on the motherfucking front porch and eating your snacks while you hunt."

Bez growled and slammed a drawer closed. This kid was trying his patience. "Leviathan—"

"I can full name you, too, Beelzebub. Now quit being a dick and accept that fact that three hours away is plenty far enough."

Bez closed his eyes, fighting to control his temper. "Fine. But not a mile closer."

"Fine. Now get your ass out there and hunt, ya lazy wanker. I've got a long drive ahead of me to get into position."

"Three hours, Levi. I'm not fucking around."

"Duh, you never do, asshole."

The phone disconnected, Levi having hung up. Bez glared at the device in his hands. As much as he loved his brothers, he found Levi to be the most challenging. He was the youngest of the seven by nearly fifty years, and he'd never really grown out of that little-brother attitude. At least not enough for Bez's preference.

With a deep breath, Bez pocketed his phone again and got back to work. There was nothing he could do about Levi, and he may need the help later. The kid was better than nothing.

Bez secured the majority of the weaponry back where it belonged before moving toward the large metal box brushing the rafters of the space. Like a shipping container made of highly polished steel, the box sat in the attic along with the closet of weapons. Both accessible only by a pull-down ladder tucked inside an access panel in the ceiling of the back hallway of the house. The attic was nearly airtight, making it difficult for even a shifter with Bez's strong senses to get a read on what was up there. Even with the access panel opened, Bez could hardly smell the scents of the floor below him.

The box turned out to be a simple but secure safe room. With a thick, steel ceiling, armored walls, and keypad entry door, there was no way even someone as strong as a wolf shifter was getting into the metal box without being allowed access. The perfect spot to stash the Omega while Bez and his team hunted the shifters who'd taken her. But first, he had to find her and get her out of the swamp. Alive.

Bez stood in the kitchen and finished his snack before drinking two bottles of water. When finished, he felt fully fueled and antsy to start his search. His wolf had been pawing at him all day, the call of the swamp too much to resist. The animal within needed to hunt, to find, to destroy. Those were his goals, his mission. Bez knew once he let the beast out, there'd be no caging him until he'd succeeded. There was no way he was stopping to rest or coming back empty-handed. He'd hunt through the swampy land for days if he needed to.

And his wolf would love every fucking second of it.

After securing the property, Bez stripped on the covered porch. The sun had dropped a bit in the last hour, marking the time as late afternoon. A time when wolves liked to be lazy and sleep. Bez could take advantage of the wolf's natural tendencies to do a little recon on the camp in the bayou, once he found it. And he would find it. There was no doubt in his mind. Blaze hadn't sent him on this mission without reason. Bez was a natural tracker, a long-time soldier in Blaze's army, and a Dire Wolf. Bigger, badder, and stronger than any other wolf shifters out there. If Blaze wanted him to find the Omega, he *would* find her. Failure was not an option.

Stretching one last time, Bez shifted to his wolf form, shaking out his fur as his paws landed on the wood planks of the porch. His senses heightened, and his brain quickly caught up with the extra input. This was it, his first chance to find the camp. He wouldn't stop searching until he had their location pinned down. Until he had eyes on the Omega.

With nothing more than a chuff, he took off across the green grass, heading for the woods.

Heading for the hunt.

Eight

"What should we do today?"

Sariel dangled her foot off the cot, letting her toes drag back and forth across the wood floor. "I was thinking of heading to the pool. Maybe soak up some sun, work on my tan, and have the cabana boys bring me margaritas all afternoon."

Angelita giggled, a sound that brought a smile to Sariel's face. "No, silly. What are we really going to do?"

Sariel's smiled dropped. "Same thing as always. Sit here and wish we weren't sitting here."

Angelita went quiet, and the room filled with a tension Sariel could feel. Shit. She hated when she lost control of her calm around Angelita. She was just a girl, a young, scared girl who needed someone to look out for her. That had become Sariel's job, and she sometimes sucked at it.

"I was just kidding," Sariel said, trying to keep her voice light. "We could play cards again."

Angelita stayed silent for a moment long enough to make Sariel's heart race. The girl had a way of seeing through everyone around her, including Sariel. If she tried too hard to be upbeat and positive, Angelita withdrew. If she tried too little, the girl would pester her until she reignited her belief that they'd get out of here. Sariel never knew what direction the girl's thoughts would go.

"You know what I want to do today?" Angelita asked in her soft voice.

Sariel turned her head to peer at the girl, assuming she'd be playing cards or checkers or something equally as mind-numbing within a few minutes. "What's that, little one?"

"I want to get off this boat."

The air in the room grew heavier, thicker than just the humidity could cause. Sariel closed her eyes and took a deep breath, putting her words together. Looking for an answer or response that made sense. That would help Angelita refocus on what they could control instead of things out of their reach.

But eventually, Sariel scoffed. They were trapped on a houseboat in the middle of a damn swamp under guard twenty-four seven. As positive as she could be, Sariel had to admit the options for escape were pretty much nonexistent. She dug deep, searching for that hope she had found just a few days before, but it was gone. Blown out by exhaustion and fear. Extinguished.

"Me too," she whispered, curling into a ball on her cot. "By the gods, Angelita. I want off this boat, too."

"If we want it bad enough, we'll get it." Angelita mimicked Sariel's position, drawing her legs up on her own cot as if to sleep. "That's what my grandpa always said. I'm an Omega, and so are you. If we want things bad enough, we'll get them."

Sariel bit her lip, wishing hard that those words were true. Knowing that sometimes, wanting things wasn't enough to actually get them.

"Want with me," Angelita said, her voice low but firm. "Let's take a nap so we can dream of all the things we're going to do when we get out of here. A shower, food, and a big, strong shifter to spend time with... remember? That's what you said. Want with me, Sariel. If we want it bad enough, we'll get it."

"I don't know if I believe all that, Angelita." Sariel slid her arm under her ratty pillow, pulling up every image and thought of what she wanted. Of all the things she'd do once they got off this fucking boat. Of simply surviving another day. She was tired, worn out by the heat and the stench and the desolation she felt. The helplessness. But she could want. If Angelita thought it would help, she would want all fucking day for the kid. She had to.

"Then I'll believe enough for both of us," Angelita said, the squeaking of her cot joining her voice as she turned over. "I'll believe, and we'll both think about all the things we want to happen."

Sariel closed her eyes, letting her thoughts fly, allowing herself to truly, utterly *want* for the first time since she'd woken up in this hellhole.

Nine

After two days and nights of scenting his way through bogs and along the banks of what seemed like an endless maze of rivers, Bez's patience finally paid off. He lay still at the base of a tree, the fur of his wolf completely covered in sticky, putrid-smelling mud. Fifty yards away sat a string of four houseboats tied together. Houseboats reeking of shifters and the decay of the swamp.

Bez spent hours curled around that tree, not moving, barely breathing as he closed off the human side of his mind and let his wolf take over. He sensed five male wolves, though only two seemed to be on the houseboats that day. The other three had left a scent trail through the brush on the spongy shore across from him. He could still see the broken grass and raised edges along the impressions in the mud from their footfalls. Bez also scented two females in residence, both shifters. The second woman concerned him, as she could be one of the male's mates. Bez had never had to kill a woman who wasn't actively trying to kill him. As progressive as he thought himself to be, the idea of killing a female just didn't sit right. But a mated pair was hard to split up, and a mated wolf would fight to the death for its other half. Bez would have to wait and see if he could determine her involvement in the outfit. Standards or no standards, no one was coming between him and the Omega.

The females were quiet through the early afternoon, rarely even speaking in the last boat to the right, while the males watched some show on a television in the far left one. Staying rooted in his spot, only moving enough to make sure his wolf scent buried under the rot of the swampy earth he covered himself in, Bez studied the setup of the enemy camp as he waited for late afternoon to come. One of the men seemed to be the leader, the hub of communication. Message alerts, phone calls, instructing his partner—the man was a bevy of information. He would be Bez's target for phase two of the mission. First, rescue the Omega. Second, capture the enemy for interrogation. That part would require he call in another of his teammates for backup, which he'd do as soon as he got the Omega back to the lake house and into that safe room. Now that he'd found her, he wasn't leaving her behind. He couldn't risk them moving her or hurting her, especially not when he was so close.

As the sun crested across the sky on a slow arc toward the invisible horizon, one man walked across the boats to the one where the women stayed. Short and squat with a choppy gait, he appeared weak to Bez—an easy kill—but Bez wouldn't underestimate him. Something had given these men the strength to take on and destroy an entire pack, whether it was skill or training or the possibility of a werewolf on their side. That feat was enough to make Bez wary.

The man lumbered up the three steps to the women's boat, stopping on the deck to look out over the water. To look exactly in the direction where Bez lay. Bez stared back, not moving, barely breathing. He had made sure to cover himself in the fetid mud of the swamp, so he doubted the man knew he was there. Between the mud and the way Bez had tucked himself against the tree, there was no way the shifter on the boat could see him or smell him. Still, he made sure to be ready to leap into a fight, just in case.

"Yo, Marcus."

Bez turned his eyes toward the second man as he appeared from inside the far left houseboat. This one, tall and lean, carried himself in a manner that made Bez's wolf take notice. Something dark and devious lurked under the surface of that shifter, and he was definitely more of a threat than the other.

The short shifter, Marcus apparently, turned. "What's up?"

"The guys will be back soon; they've got the beast with them."

Bez nearly growled, his stomach burning. Damn it, they'd actually found a werewolf. Or at least, that's what he assumed the man meant by beast. If that assumption proved true, the Omega was in more danger than he'd thought. Werewolves were nearly impossible to kill without beheading, stronger in their wolfish form than most shifters, and able to hide as humans for the vast majority of the month. But when that full moon hung bright in the sky, they brought hell upon any female shifter nearby. Omega or not.

"So what's the plan?" Marcus asked, pulling Bez's attention back to the fuckers on deck.

"Tonight, we keep it boxed here. We're probably going to need to find a human female for the thing to eat; can't go giving him the big meal just yet." The guy smirked, a look that made Bez's wolf want to snarl and challenge him even as he fought to remain still and hidden. "Tomorrow, you take the Omega bitch north with Vreel while Chance and I take the beast to Thunderhead. A full day in the van with the dud ought to turn his crank enough to finish off those mountain men after what they did to Zacor. Even if she isn't exactly whole."

"Whole?" Marcus asked. Bez inched his nose forward, wondering the same thing.

"Yeah," the taller man said, his grin growing wide and hungry. "Gotta keep the blood flowing for him. Easiest way to do that is to cut a little off at a time."

Bez clenched his teeth, holding back a snarl. He hadn't even known the other shifter would be there, but he still felt the sickening sense of guilt at the thought of having to leave her behind when he grabbed the Omega. But his orders were set, and without a second man with him, there was no way he could ensure the safety of the Omega while protecting two women. He'd just have to hope he and his team could get back to the camp in time to help her. He'd be happy to let Thaus loose on the kidnappers once he got the information Blaze wanted. Sick fuckers, this lot.

The tall man glanced at his phone as it pinged. "The moon will start to rise in a few hours. You ever seen one of these monsters feed?"

Marcus shook his head.

"You're in for a real show, my friend. These beasts are a fucking treat. Go nap with the bitches, keep them from getting too chummy. As soon as the moon is high, we'll have to hunt down some female human flesh." The man laughed and walked back into the houseboat, immediately starting a conversation on his phone. Marcus disappeared into the houseboat where the women slept. Bez waited for any sounds from him or the women. It took a moment, but Marcus seemed to find a comfortable spot to "guard" the women. There was a creak, a sigh, and then just the soft, even breathing and slow heartbeat that indicated sleep broke the gentle song of the swamp-loving insects. Three sleeping, one talking loudly on his phone about some human sporting event. One hunting.

Seeing a perfect opportunity, and knowing his time was limited as the others were on their way to the camp, Bez crawled out of the mud and slithered on his belly toward the houseboats. He inched across boggy ground until he reached the water's edge then slipped underneath the black surface, silently rearranging bone and muscle while suspended underwater. In his human form, Bez swam to the side of the boat, completely submerged, refusing to make a single ripple that could give away his position.

Once Bez reached his destination, he mounted the side of the houseboat. Arms stretching and toes supporting, he scaled the metal structure silently, unconcerned with his nudity. The three heartbeats inside beat slow and steady, the breathing just as calm. His first target slept soundly in the company of the two females, making things easier on Bez. The tall male was at least two houseboats over, his laughter interrupting the slosh of the water against the side of the boats. He'd abandoned his phone call while Bez was under water, instead watching some sort of laugh track backed show on his television. Bez clung to the side of the boat and readied himself to move. The loud volume of the show was certainly enough to cover any errant sounds Bez made while extracting the Omega. He was almost thankful to the bastard down the way. Way to make his job easier.

Pulling himself up to the window by his fingertips, Bez peeked through the filthy glass. The two women lay in cots at opposite sides of the room, while the man leaned back in a chair by the door as he rested. Bez's eyes traveled over each woman, wondering which the Omega was. He guessed the dark-haired one on the left as his eyes kept coming back to her. Drawn to her. His instincts letting him know she was what he wanted.

Silently, he slid open the screen and crawled through the open window. He flinched at the smell of the place, sweat and fear and something dirty lingering in the still air. Something worse than the swamp outside. Jesus, how long had the second woman been there?

He landed softly on the wooden floor, his bare feet helping to keep the sounds to a minimum. There was no going back now. He had to eliminate the guard in the room and extricate the Omega. And he had to do it without alerting the other shifter down the way.

All in a day's work, really.

He stepped with care, his movements subtle and deliberate as he snuck across the room toward the guard, the man named Marcus. His eyes lighted upon the woman on his left over and over. She pulled his focus, demanded his attention even in her sleep. But Bez had one job to do first. Before he could grab the Omega, he needed to eliminate the threat. And Marcus, as slow and weak as he appeared, was a threat.

Pulling his wolf forward and letting his fingers shift to claws, Bez walked up behind the sleeping shifter. Silent, barely causing the air to react. He stepped close enough to smell the man, close enough to feel the heat radiating from his body. Raising his hands, Bez brought them in front of the man's throat. Ready...able... determined. In a single, smooth system of movements, Bez grabbed Marcus' chin and sliced his throat with nothing but his claws and brute strength. The man had no time to react, no time to fight back. Still, Bez held Marcus in a paralyzing hold as his blood, his ability to shift and regenerate, ran down the front of his chest. It took a handful of precious seconds, but Bez remained in position until death washed over the man. Until the threat to the Omega was neutralized.

Once Marcus' heart pumped for the last time, Bez turned his attention to the women. The lighter-haired one smelled of salt and sadness, making Bez think she'd cried herself to sleep. The act of a young woman. The other one smelled of sweetness and light, of spice and warmth—an intriguing scent that teased him in ways he'd never experienced. The lighter had to be the younger of the two, and most definitely his Omega, but the older, darker shewolf held his attention, making his head swivel in her direction every other second.

Fucking distractions.

Giving in to his instincts, Bez slipped closer to where the raven-haired woman slept. His wolf prowled along the edges of his mind, interest piqued by the attraction Bez felt to the woman. Obsessed with her shape and smell.

Bez inched his way across the boat, moving silently toward the woman. He couldn't look away from her, wouldn't have wanted to. Something about her… something important spoke to him. Exploded his senses and ensnared his mind. She was witchcraft and heaven, the lure of sin and the forgiveness of faith all rolled up into one dark-haired package. It infuriated Bez, made him wary of her presence. What was this power she had over him to distract him from his mission? Who the hell was she and what was she even doing in this dump?

All questions he and his wolf had to know the answers to.

Bez stopped right next to her cot, his knee brushing the wood frame. The need to touch her brought out more of his human side, made him feel things he hadn't in…well, perhaps ever. Mission delayed, focus shifted from saving the Omega to this unknown being before him, he felt his world spinning slightly off-kilter. And he liked it.

Unable to resist for a single second more, he leaned down slowly, his body tense, sweat forming on his brow. He had to see her, had to know what—

Her eyes opened, the color dark and deep, meeting his in a stare that sent him soaring. Everything, every piece and particle of Bez's life, stopped, shifted, and reset. With one look, the woman lodged herself into his heart, deep within his very soul. His human side shoved his wolf to the back, demanding his space to comprehend what this all meant. The wolf knew, though. The wolf had always known.

She stared with eyes the color of coffee, with a look of peace and understanding dancing across her pretty face. And she took ownership of him. She offered Bez no escape, no chance to refuse her. She simply became his, and he became hers.

His wolf howled in his head, rejoicing at having found her, singing his song of completeness. Happy to finally be mated.

Mated.

Bez couldn't breathe, couldn't look away. This was his *mate.* Instincts long forgotten in place of strategy and fighting styles flared to life, the bond joining him to this unknown shifter wrapping around his heart and pulling his thoughts away from the mission. None of the Dire Wolves had found their mates, the pack of seven existing instead to fight and kill and hunt. But this woman, this bond, had suddenly made his existence…

Tactile. Real. Significant.

Beautiful brown eyes looked up at him, deep and soulful, eyes he wanted to look into until the day he died. Which very well could be that day if he didn't pull himself together. She blinked once, twice, and then those eyes went wide and her heart jumped. Belatedly, Bez remembered he was naked, covered in mud and filth and blood, and standing over a woman he'd never met. Not exactly the most calming of sights. Without pause, he placed his hand over her mouth to hold in her scream, shivering at the feel of her flesh against his. Even if she was trying to bite him.

"Stop. I'm not here to hurt you," he hissed, keeping his voice little more than air. "I'm here to save the Omega. President Blasius Zenne sent me."

The woman stilled, looking worried and fearful. Bez hated that he scared her, hated that he couldn't comfort her in some way, but those instincts were new. He was there to save, not soothe. Finally, his mate swallowed and nodded. She held his gaze as she gripped his wrist, pulling his hand from her mouth.

"Which Omega?"

Bez liked the sound of her voice, dark and deep, filled with a sensual tone. It called to him, left him speechless as it danced across his ears. But then he cocked his head, her words finally filtering through the haze.

"Pardon?"

"Which Omega…? There are two of us."

Motherfucker. Bez felt his eyes go wide and his heart make a single, solitary slam against his chest. Of all the fucking luck. Two Omegas, two targets. If he'd known there would be two women to extricate, he'd have brought a second man to secure the second captive. That was basic policy on reverse kidnappings. One Dire per kidnappee. But now—

The woman's face fell, her lips forming a thin line, and her eyes went soft. "I see. You're here for Angelita?"

Bez nodded, slow and heavy. "The pup."

"Then I suggest you get at it." She threw a glance toward the door, gasping when she saw the fallen shifter. "Oh. Okay. Oh, God, he's dead, isn't he?"

Bez watched his mate as she visibly withdrew from the dead body of Marcus. For the first time in his life, he regretted killing something the way he had. Not for the loss of life, but for the way his mate seemed repulsed by it.

The woman finally looked away, closing her eyes tightly for a moment before turning that dark stare on him. "You need to take her, now. Before they come for her. I overheard something about moving her north. She's just a baby, and what these animals intend to do with her would break her very soul."

Bez's wolf wanted to growl, but he held it back. It was recon time, not fight time. Not yet. "What are they planning?"

"I don't know for sure, but it has to be bad." Her eyes grew more worried, her frown turning into a scowl. "They call me the dud because I'm infertile. What does that tell you about their plans?"

The idea of other shifters forcing themselves on his mate snapped his carefully cultivated control. Bez growled, long and loud and unrestrained. The sick fucks deserved to die horrible, painful deaths—ones he'd be thrilled to visit upon them.

The woman glanced to where the young girl slept. "Don't scare her. She's young and extremely naïve. You need to take her right now. Get her the hell out of here before the rest of the men come back."

By the gods, the fates didn't mess around. She was perfect for him, so strong, so brave. And so smart— Bez knew she was right. He needed to haul ass and get the younger Omega out of danger, but he didn't want to leave this woman's side. He willed his legs to move, his body to respond, but his mind and heart and wolf were set. He couldn't ignore the mating bond, couldn't dare fail her. Just the thought of walking away without her by his side gutted him.

Bez shook his head and sighed. "I don't—"

The sound of the other man in camp yelling for Marcus woke Bez from his mate-induced distraction. Fuck, he needed to *go*. Grab the young Omega and run. But this woman was his *mate*, his one and only, and he would have to leave her behind to be able to get the other Omega out as per the plan. His training told him to leave his mate, to grab the target, secure her, and call in a second team to come back to the houseboat camp. But he knew that wouldn't work. The men would whisk his mate away before he and his team could make it back, leaving him chasing trails and ghosts until he tracked her down. And he would track her down. He was the best tracker anyone had ever seen, impossible to shake or outrun. But what could happen to her in the interim made Bez's blood run cold. No. He couldn't abandon her. Couldn't risk her.

The thought strengthened his resolve and made his brain spin off on a secondary plan. For the first time in his very long life, he would not be following policies, procedures, or orders. He would not be working under the mantle of anyone else. He didn't want to leave his mate behind.

So he wouldn't.

Grabbing his mate's arm, he pulled her out of the cot. "We go. Now."

"But you're only here for her."

Bez yanked her to her feet, harder than he wanted to but needing her to *move*. "Not anymore."

She gave him a hard look, obviously doubting him. Something that almost made him smile. He'd show her, teach her—the last thing she should do was doubt a Dire Wolf.

Bez held out a hand, backing toward where the

younger Omega, Angelita, still slept, inviting his mate to follow him. She stared at him thoughtfully, her expression filled with a meaning Bez couldn't figure out. But he wanted to, and he would. Someday. After he'd taken the time to learn everything there was to know about her. But that time wasn't right then, and the place definitely wasn't this shitty houseboat camp.

"Please," he whispered, begging for what had to be the first time in his life. Something that finally got a reaction from his mate. She glanced at his hand once… twice…before taking a deep breath.

And then she grabbed hold of him.

Ignoring the tingles the simple touch sent shooting up his arm, Bez pulled her beside him. He loved the scent of her, wanted to breathe her in for days, but there was no time. The two hurried across the floor to where the younger Omega slept. Considering the reaction his mate had to him standing over her, he let her take the lead. He didn't want to scare the girl and alert the other shifter. Bez stood guard as his mate knelt down next to the cot and brushed Angelita's hair off her forehead.

"C'mon, hon. It's time to go."

The voice of the other guard grew closer, the pitch displaying his irritation when Marcus didn't answer. Not that he could have. Though, the tall one had no way of knowing the man lay dead on the floor, but he would soon.

Angelita opened her eyes, jumping back against the wall when she saw Bez. Before she could scream, his mate put her hand over the girl's mouth and leaned close to whisper in her ear.

"He's here to help us. We're leaving. Right now."

It took the younger Omega barely a second to understand the words. Once she did, she hopped out of the bed and grabbed his mate's hand. Clinging to one another, the two women looked up at him, ready but questioning. Wanting to leave but obviously afraid.

"What do we do now?" his mate asked. Bez didn't want her to see what he was about to do, but he couldn't lie to her. So he didn't.

"You two hide. I kill the guard. Then we run."

Ten

Sariel stared at the man who'd woken her, unable to form words. He planned on killing the guard…in front of her and Angelita. Her hands shook with the adrenaline racing through her bloodstream, and her skin felt clammy beneath the cotton tank top and shorts she'd donned for her nap. He terrified her with his casual cruelty, and yet her body yearned for him, demanding she move closer. The strength of the wolf inside her was the only thing keeping her from going into shock. Her mate…this man was her *mate*. Huge and beastly, with the lightest, fiercest eyes she'd ever seen, he stood before her talking about killing a shifter as if it were just another item on his to-do list. Which Sariel guessed it technically was.

But he was her *mate*.

When she'd first realized that fact, lying in the cot as he loomed over her in the shadows, she thought the fates were mocking her. Assuming he worked with the men who'd stolen her from her home, her stomach had roiled in dread. Thankfully, the fates had been kind, not cruel. They'd sent her a mate who was strong and powerful, near-savage it seemed. Not one who'd already done so much harm to her. They'd sent her exactly the man she needed.

And she wasn't going to squander this opportunity.

"C'mon, kid. Let's get out of the way." She gripped Angelita's hand and dragged her farther back, giving her mate room to do what he needed to. She'd told the girl they'd get out of this hell. If this man, this big beast of a shifter the fates had sent to her as her destined soul mate, was willing to help them, so be it. She knew she could trust the man fated for her. The man watching her with eyes she almost couldn't tear her own away from.

Her heart skipped as he stared, as words defining their bond echoed in her head. Fated...mated... claimed. Her mate had found her. What a massive bit of craziness to add to this screwed-up situation. She'd met her mate while being held hostage in a houseboat in the middle of a swamp. That should have been the plot of some crazy movie, not reality. And yet, he'd shown up to save them. Well, technically, he'd shown up to save Angelita. She was more of a complication to him, it seemed. The thought of him leaving her behind, taking only Angelita and rescuing the young girl as he'd planned, had made her sick at first. Even sicker than assuming he was one of the men who'd kidnapped her in the first place. She didn't want to be left behind. She couldn't stand to live another second in this prison, especially now that she'd glimpsed a way out. She would have followed them if she'd had to. But she didn't have to—he seemed just as against leaving her behind as she felt about being left.

The sound of approaching footsteps caught Sariel's attention a second behind her mystery man. He turned his ice-blue eyes toward the noise in a move that was pure predator, all animal...totally hot in a weird he's-strong-enough-to-take-on-my-enemies sort of way. And as much as she almost didn't want to admit it, that level of aggression and protectiveness *was* hot. She'd been cooped up for weeks, terrified the men guarding her would hurt her in some way other than the mental torture that delighted them, and unable to figure a way out for her and Angelita. Screw her independent nature, her mate had shown up, big and bad and looking like a monster in the dim light, but he was ready to save her. She could fight her own battles another day. Right then, she wanted nothing more than to hop on that white horse of his and let him lead them all off into the sunset.

Or through the swamp, as the case seemed to be.

"Marcus," the approaching guard yelled from outside. "Wake your lazy ass up." The footsteps grew louder.

Sariel's mate motioned for her and Angelita to move farther back, away from the door. Sariel dragged Angelita to the corner, crouching down and wrapping herself around the younger girl. He watched them, his eyes on hers, until he seemed satisfied that Sariel and Angelita were settled into a good spot.

Without warning, he stalked to the door, angling his head toward the sound of the approaching guard. There was something beautiful in his harsh extremes, something sexy in the way he let his inner animal rule his body. He reeked of shifter with very little of his human side shining through. That fact alone had her fixated on him, had her wolf practically hunting him. Wanting him.

Taller than most shifters or human men she'd known, he stood just behind the door, his head brushing the low ceiling. He curled his broad shoulders into a hunting pose, the muscles corded across his back. His thighs tight with anticipation. Pure and utter hunter.

He cocked his shorn head as the guard's footsteps hit the deck of the second houseboat, ready and definitely able to fight. Moonlight shone through the open window, bathing him in a silvery glow. She assumed he was blond based solely on his lighter eyebrows and the hair leading down from his navel, not that it mattered. He was big and bold, larger than life, his body screaming of masculinity. And he was about to kill a man while she watched, to save them all.

Grabbing Angelita and turning her head away from the door, Sariel angled her body to protect the girl from what she knew was about to happen. Her mate had been sent here for the younger woman, and though Sariel hadn't been a consideration of the rescue, she was grateful for him. She couldn't have saved the girl on her own. She would have tried and tried hard, but she doubted she would have succeeded. Sariel would happily help keep the younger Omega safe so he could fulfill whatever plans Blasius Zenne had tasked him with.

The footsteps grew closer, the guard's stride gaining speed. Her mate gave her one last look over his shoulder before he crouched into a pouncing position. Every inch of him hard and tense, ready. Able. Savage.

The guard kicked the door open at the exact same moment the blue-eyed stranger struck. Sariel barely had a chance to see what happened because her mate moved so fast. The door had only just opened when her mate's hand slashed across the guard's throat, his other arm pushing the man to the floor as blood sprayed from his neck. Before Sariel could even take a breath, her mate turned—eyes glowing, chest heaving—and looked right at her. She could feel the tension between them, relished in the tightening of the bond. The connection to him. Her mate had killed for her. Had protected her and the young one they were responsible for. He'd proven himself as a strong and able male. God, that was exceptionally sexy in a very primal, animalistic kind of way.

"We go. Now." His words were an order, almost nothing more than a grunt. Sariel nodded. She may have been strong with the power of her Omega, but this beast was a totally different animal. He could raze the world if he needed to, and she knew it. She sensed it. That knowledge made something ancient and carnal burn through her blood, a form of attraction that had her growling low and soft. Her mate responded with his own growl, his light eyes following her as she stood and moved closer. But before Sariel could take more than a few steps, Angelita grabbed her hand, pulling her out of the moment.

"What do we do?" Angelita asked, sounding slightly panicked. Understandably so.

Sariel stared into the fiery eyes of her mate, refusing to look away even as she sensed how much more wolf than man he was at that moment. "We do whatever he says. We follow him from here on out."

The man grunted, still watching her. She felt more than saw his wolf surge, those eyes going from washed-out aquamarine to bright silver and back. The color spinning in a way that pinged something in her memory. Something she'd learned about but never seen.

She faltered, unable to hold his gaze a second longer. The moment had gotten too intense, the pull to him too hard to resist. She had to break the spell.

"Now what?" she whispered when she was finally able to look up from the floor. He glanced from Sariel to Angelita, eyes hard and face giving nothing away, before motioning them over to the far side of the houseboat.

"Up and out, ladies."

Not what she was expecting, but she didn't refuse. The three slipped out the window, dropping into the swamp below. Sariel hated the feeling of the water surrounding her. Hated even more knowing there were things beneath the surface that could be more predator than she was. Though she doubted they were more predator than her mate.

Sariel swam and waded her way through the dark water and mucky riverbed, trudging on until they reached a spot of land dry enough to gain their footing. She stumbled up the grassy land first, holding on to Angelita's hand and pulling her along.

"I never want to go swimming again," Sariel said with a shiver. Her mate stalked out of the swamp, staring at her as if she were something to eat… to devour. And by the gods, she wanted that man to devour her. Droplets of water, mud, and muck clinging to every curve of his body, running down the length of it. Accentuating every hard muscle. She bit her lip and shivered, pulling at her sodden clothes. "What now?"

Her mate took a moment to investigate their location, looking all around them and even up to the sky. Sariel mimicked him, though she doubted she saw the things he did. Still, it was a joy to be standing outside underneath the night sky again. The moon hung heavy, on its way to its pinnacle. Full moons always made her twitchy, made her inner animal itch to be released. Tonight was no different. Hell, the moon affected humans every month. It certainly affected shifters just as much.

"They're coming back." Her mate looked out across the water they'd crossed, his eyes sharp and his chest still as he held his breath. He glared into the distance, a steely determination on his face. "We need to run."

"As wolf or human?"

He turned to her, his eyes blue once more. "Wolf."

Sariel pulled her tank top over her head, glad to be rid of the sticky, wet fabric. The night air felt amazing against her skin, for once the humidity a benefit instead of an irritation. Her mate watched her, his eyes following her hands as she dropped them to the waistband of her shorts. She hooked her thumbs beneath the elastic and slid them over her hips. The weight of the water pulled them down her legs, and they fell to the grass with a muffled splat. Sariel kicked them off, standing on the balls of her feet, and stretched.

"God, I've missed my wolf." She wanted to dance

in the night, celebrate being released from her cage, but she knew there was no time. Still, she stood brazen and bold, completely naked in front of her mate, and let the slight breeze blowing through the trees caress her body as it hadn't in months. Her mate watched her, stared at her, ate her up with his eyes. His gaze slid over every curve of her body, head to toe, almost as if he was memorizing her. Every inch of her felt that stare, responding as if to touch. Nipples hard, goose bumps rising, Sariel held still and let her mate *see* her as she waited to let her wolf free.

"I can't." The little voice may as well have been a bucket of ice water thrown over Sariel. She and her mate turned in an odd sort of unison, both staring at an extremely uncomfortable-looking Angelita.

"What do you mean, you can't?" Sariel asked.

"I can't shift on command. I've never been able to."

Her mate growled as the sound of an engine grew in the distance. "Our wolves have a better chance in this swamp." He turned those glowing eyes on Angelita, the power of his inner wolf making the air feel electrified. "Shift to your wolf."

Angelita whimpered and shook her head. "I can't."

The thump of car doors closing reached Sariel's sensitive ears, and her heart raced as she watched the showdown between man and girl.

"Omega, you need to shift. Now."

Angelita met Sariel's concerned gaze, her eyes wide

with fear. "I can't. I swear, I can't. If I try, I'll fail. I can't even feel my wolf spirit right now."

Sariel looked to her mate, ready to follow his lead. He gave her a heated once-over, his eyes resting on her chest for a long second before meeting her own.

"Shift."

With a nod, Sariel shifted to her wolf form, sinking fast to the gray wolf of her second form. The man went still, eyes wide as he looked off in the direction of the houseboats. The scent of something rotten and wrong met Sariel's nose, and she shook her head to try to rid herself of the stench. The man breathed deeper, nostrils flaring, hands clenching into fists.

"Motherfucker," he hissed, turning back to the women. "Do you smell that, Omega? Do you sense the wrongness of the monster?"

Angelita nodded, her eyes bouncing from the man to the darkness behind him.

"That's the scent of werewolf, little one. Real, honest to God, beasts of the moon, werewolves."

Angelita gasped and took a step back as Sariel whined, desperate to run. There weren't a lot of things that could make her feel the level of terror currently winding around her heart, but the presence of a werewolf was certainly one of them. Half dead, rotting away under the full moons, werewolves were the epitome of all that was wrong with an animal and human mix. They hunted relentlessly, killed indiscriminately, and wreaked havoc for three nights whenever the full moon lit up the sky. The way it did that night. And—the most terrifying fact of all to her—they only hunted female shifters. They attacked mercilessly, sometimes wiping out every female in a pack in one night, feeding off the bodies of the fallen women. A fact that led most shewolves to run for their lives when the beasts showed up. And damn, did Sariel want to run. But she wanted to bring Angelita with her.

"Omega," the man said, the stiff set of his jaw the only outward sign of the tension that had to be nearly suffocating him. "We have to—"

"I can't!" Angelita exclaimed, her breaths coming so fast, Sariel worried the girl would hyperventilate.

Sariel whined and rubbed her side along Angelita's legs, pushing her fur against the girl's skin, wishing it was enough to get her to reach her wolf spirit. But Angelita stood, human as ever, trembling and gasping in her fright. Sariel had one terrifying moment when her mate turned away from them, thinking he'd run off and leave Angelita behind. But she should have known better.

With a growl, her mate grabbed Angelita around her waist, hauling her off her feet. The girl yelped as he tossed her on his back and began to move, strides long and aggressive. In two steps, he morphed from man to animal, his sterling wolf form taller and longer than her own. A huge, uniquely colored beast that almost made her stop in her tracks.

A Dire Wolf.

Assumed extinct, Dire Wolves had been the gladiators of the shifter world. Their size and strength were legendary, their fierceness in battle told in stories over campfires and with a sense of respect, of reverence and fear. But Dires were extinct—no one had seen one for over two hundred years. Until tonight, of course. The size of him, the heaviness of his muscles, the breadth of his shoulders, and the unique ermine spots along his back and haunches revealed her mate for what he truly was. A beast of battle; a weapon in the war on the worst of the things that went bump in the night. Untamed, unbeatable, and uncontrollable.

Oh hell, what had the fates been thinking?

Eleven

Her mate ran hard and fast across the swamplands. Sariel followed, struggling to keep pace but refusing to slow him down. Angelita clung to his thick neck with her eyes squeezed shut. Sariel wished she could comfort the girl, could tell her things would be okay, but as the sound of men's voices reached their ears, even she doubted.

They yelled and hollered, splashing through the water behind her. Sariel ran harder, desperate to put distance between her and her captors. Her mate growled with every stride, his paws eating up the earth under their feet.

And then the howling began. Deep and dark, it was not a sound a shifter would make. The call of a werewolf on the hunt. She whimpered on the second howl, stumbled on the third. Once she regained her footing, her mate edged closer, brushing his shoulder against hers with every step. Supporting her with his touch. Sariel took what comfort she could from his presence and ran harder.

Sariel and her mate raced through the woods along the riverbank, paws flying across the swampy earth. She followed his lead, stretching her body to keep up as best she could over the difficult terrain. The sounds of the animals chasing them were enough to make her want to run faster, though, so she did. She was determined to escape. To live.

About an hour into their run, deep in a wilderness that made Sariel's hackles rise, Angelita pulled the man to a stop.

"I think I'm ready now," she said.

Sariel's mate shifted to his human form, dropping to one knee in front of the girl so he could look her in the eye. "We must hurry, Omega. Shift."

Angelita closed her eyes and curled her hands into fists. For several minutes, she struggled, trying to pull her inner wolf forward. Sariel waited and watched, her heart breaking for the girl. Shifting forms, while natural, still took time to learn. It took strength and mental skill to access the magic of their kind. Angelita wasn't ready yet.

The Dire glanced at Sariel before placing a hand on Angelita's arm, stopping her.

"Omega, we need to keep moving."

"I can do this."

"No, I don't think you can."

"Yes." Angelita's eyes went dark, her shoulders back and her hands in fists. "I'll show you. I just need a minute."

The man glanced around the woods. "We don't have a minute."

"I can do this on my own." Angelita's voice rose, almost yelling at the man.

He glared at her, eyes streaked with liquid silver and glowing. "Then shift, Omega."

"Give me a minute," Angelita cried, her face red.

"There is no time for waiting; we must move." He grabbed her arm at the elbow and placed his other hand on her forehead. "Shift, now."

Sariel took a step back, growling at the energy she sensed surging from the earth. Angelita's eyes went wide as what felt an awful lot like some kind of bastardized Alpha-order exploded into the clearing. She dropped her head back, body tense as the force around her brought her to her toes, pulling her up. Bending her body to someone else's will. Angelita's jaw fell open, her throat working as if to scream, but no sound came out. She was silent, stretched and taut and screaming her agony in her own mind.

Slowly, Angelita began to change, bones and muscles rearranging themselves into a lupine shape.

The girl trembled, body tense, fighting every alteration. Sariel whimpered as she watched, horrified. Changing so slowly would be painful—more than just painful, it would be torture. She couldn't take bearing witness to it any longer.

Sariel shifted human, yelling to Angelita even before she'd fully made the switch. "Relax, don't fight it. It won't hurt so much if you stop fighting."

Angelita's head fell to the side, her eyes meeting Sariel's. Looking tired and so very frightened.

The older shifter nodded, giving the girl a small smile. "It'll be okay; just fall into it. Let your wolf take over. She'll protect you."

As Angelita began to shift faster, closing her eyes and allowing her wolf to push through, Sariel walked to the side of her mate. His body tensed as she approached, his eyes locked on the shifting form of the younger girl. Sariel saw his regret in the clench of his jaw, the tic of a muscle near his eye. He hadn't meant for Angelita's shift to go so wrong.

Not able to stand seeing him in distress, Sariel walked right up beside him, purposely brushing her shoulder against his arm. He jerked and looked down, obviously surprised when her skin met his. Sariel waited, watching him, continuing to touch him in her subtle way. Wolves, as pack animals, relied on touch; they needed it. Touch from a packmate could calm the nerves or lessen a bout of sadness. Her mate acted as if he didn't like to be touched, but Sariel knew differently. The need for physical contact was part of who they were, in their nature. Touch healed.

Sariel stayed where she was, leaning into his arm until he sighed and pressed back. Taking comfort and giving it, all at the same time. She smiled up at him before leaning her head against his bicep and looking back to where Angelita stood. And then they waited for the young girl to finish the longest shift Sariel had ever seen.

Once fully wolf, Angelita fell to the grassy floor of the forest. Sariel followed, shifting without moving away from her mate, brushing her fur against his leg as she waited. Angelita's red wolf was petite but obviously strong, with a lean yet muscular physique. Sariel could tell she'd be able to handle the run once she physically recovered from that horrible shift. Recovering mentally would be a different story.

It took Angelita several seconds to be able to push to her feet, her chest still heaving and her legs wobbly. She looked exhausted. Sariel hurried to her, nuzzling and whining at the little wolf. Trying to give the girl the support she obviously needed. Her mate shifted back to his animal form as well, the wolves huddling together to comfort their youngest member.

Sariel's mate was the first to break contact, moving a few steps away and scenting the air around them for signs of danger. There was no rot drifting with the breeze, no sound of a beast coming after them through the woods. Still, Sariel worried. Her mate must have as well because, with a huff and a quiet yip, he ran ahead, the two shewolves immediately following him through the night. Sariel stayed next to Angelita, refusing to take even one step in front of the girl. She would not allow Angelita to be left behind.

Eventually, the man led them to a dusty old Jeep with gigantic tires parked along a stretch of road so rough and buried in the trees, she doubted most people even knew it was there. Perhaps a service road or fire stop. Whatever it was, she'd never been happier to see a vehicle in her entire life. Especially one that looked made for off-roading.

Her mate shifted as they approached the Jeep, never breaking stride while he went from four feet to two. Sariel followed, cracking her neck as skin replaced fur. Angelita stayed wolf, probably too afraid of getting stuck in her human form to shift back.

Naked and dirty, Sariel and her mate hurried to the Jeep with Angelita padding along behind them. Sariel held open the passenger door for the wolf, giving Angelita enough room to jump into the backseat before hopping into the front.

As her mate turned the key that had been left in the ignition, he glanced at Sariel. She could only imagine what a sight she had to be. Naked, filthy, covered in muck and God knew what else from the swamp. Not exactly pinup material. She fidgeted in her seat, crossing her legs and bringing her hands to her knees. She'd never been uncomfortable naked before, never really thought about it, as wolf shifters tended to be naked a lot. But this was different. This was her mate, and he was seeing her not just naked, but a mess.

What she wouldn't give for that day-long shower right then.

Finally, her mate looked away, easing some of the strain on Sariel's nerves. "There's a blanket and a pack of clothes in the back if you can reach them." He slammed on the gas as he spoke, the tires kicking up dirt as they raced down the road.

Sariel reached behind her, grabbing a blanket to wrap around herself and tossing a small cylinder of fabric at him. "This is all that's back there."

He unwrapped the fabric, unrolling a shirt and a pair of ratty camouflage shorts that looked as if they'd come from some kind of uniform pants. He handed her the clothes, barely flicking a glance her way. She fingered the edge of the shorts fabric, suddenly nervous.

"Um, here." She handed him the shorts, trying hard not to stare at his naked body. Trying and failing. He was so cut, so ridiculously muscled. But even that couldn't describe him fully. The man was simply big… tall and broad, muscular and strong. A solid wall of wolf shifter.

She couldn't help but let her eyes wander over

his hands as they wrapped around the steering wheel, down his rigid arms, to the rounded muscles of his shoulders. His jaw clenched as she inspected him; as her eyes traveled from his chin to his nose, back down along his neck to his chest. Lower still, over the curves and ripples of his abs, dancing along his Adonis belt before straying to where his thick penis rested against his thigh. Big, like him. Blunt and fat. Sariel shivered but took a deep breath, fighting off the wave of arousal seeing him so free and naked caused. While she watched, his penis twitched, growing fuller with every second. Mesmerized, she stared, her mouth falling open, her breathing coming faster. Good Lord, he was just so *thick*.

They hit a rough bump in the road, causing the Jeep to jerk hard to one side. Sariel ripped her eyes away from her mate's lap, her cheeks heating when she found him staring at her. Watching her. Knowing what she was looking at and probably how it made her feel. The mating haze was strong, the bond demanding. It didn't matter that they were literally running for their lives or that there was another person in the back seat. She wanted him, and she knew he could sense the desire pouring off of her.

He gave her a hard look, his eyes dropping to her legs for a moment before turning his attention back to the road. Without a second glance, he reached for the shorts, brushing his rough fingers lightly across the backs of her hands, and placed the fabric across his lap.

"Put the shirt on."

His voice felt like a reprimand, one that made Sariel's confidence backslide. Stomach sinking and face burning hotter than before, she did as she was told and pulled on the shirt. There was a hole in the side, small and perfectly round, but at least the fabric covered her to the middle of her thighs. Long and gray and soft, smelling like her mate, the shirt was a simple point of comfort. One she clung to. Once appropriately covered, she turned her body toward the passenger door and did her best to ignore the man less than a foot away. The one she sensed was trying hard to ignore her as well as he tugged the shorts up his long legs while driving.

What seemed like hours later, they pulled up outside a small house on a lakeshore. Her mate let the Jeep slide to a stop out front and then reached into the glove box to grab what looked like a black cell phone. Before she could ask, he jumped out of the vehicle, leaving her behind. Sariel sat and watched him leave, her heart thumping and her stomach sick. She had no idea where they were and why they weren't driving farther out of the area. And she had no clue how to even speak to a man like her mate. Shouldn't she at least be able to find *something* to say?

When the women didn't follow him, he slowed and turned, raising an eyebrow at Sariel as she waited in the Jeep with Angelita.

"Come." He motioned for them to follow.

Well, perhaps the inability to string words together was a problem on both their sides. Sariel crawled down from the huge vehicle, helping Angelita to the ground before walking in his direction. He watched her approach, looking her over, his eyes trailing along her body in a way that was blatantly sexual. The fire in his gaze put her body on alert, making butterflies explode in her stomach. But then he shook his head, furrowing his brow, and Sariel's excitement crashed back down to earth. Damn, she didn't know where to begin with him.

Without a word, he turned and stalked toward the house. Sariel hurried to keep up with his long stride as Angelita raced past, still in wolf form. He took the three stairs in a single step, his eyes on his phone. Couldn't he at least pay them some attention before doing… whatever it was he was doing?

"What now?" she asked as she stepped on the porch.

Her mate used a keypad to unlock the front door and led them inside, already listening to the ringing of his phone call. "We hole up and call for backup."

"We're not running?"

"If we run, they'll chase. I'd rather fight them on my terms than theirs."

Sariel glanced at Angelita, who sat on the floor watching them. Damn, she wanted to trust him, trust the man who'd come to help them, but she also wanted to get far away from this place.

"How can you be sure they'll follow us here?"

He snorted, not looking at her. "Because you two are here. They'll come."

Sariel was about to respond when Bez held up his hand, shushing her with one finger.

"The target has been acquired. I'm going to need backup." His body went still as he listened, his voice growing rougher when he spoke again. "Negative. There isn't time." He glanced at a clock and sighed. "Understood."

Sariel followed him through the house as he hung up and repocketed his phone. "So we're bait? We're just going to sit here and wait for them to come and take us again?"

His cool eyes met hers, hard and direct, not a single sign of affection or mate bond present. "They'll come, and they'll try to recapture or kill the two of you. But they won't succeed. My orders are clear—save the Omega at all costs."

"But you've already broken your orders," Sariel whispered, a knot forming in her stomach. "Save the Omega...singular. You brought me along when you should have left me and just taken Angelita. She's your mission."

His jaw clenched, a tic forming along the edge. "Strategical decision."

Sariel crossed her arms over her chest and lifted her

chin, unable to hide the shake in her voice. "And what about me?"

He stared at her for a moment, icy eyes harsh. Unwavering, unemotional…and uninterested. "You're not part of the plan."

Twelve

Bez watched his mate's face fall, an unfamiliar sensation in his gut telling him something he'd done had caused her pain. He hated that look, the way her eyes went dead and flat, and how her spark disappeared. It made her seem almost dead inside, and though he didn't know exactly how he'd messed up, the last thing Bez wanted was to see her dead in any way.

He searched for the words that would fix his mistake, that would take that look off her face, but he had none. And by the way her shoulders rolled forward in defeat, she knew it. Damn it, why did he have to find her *now*? After all the years alone, centuries upon centuries of living the life of a nomad with his Dire Wolf brothers, he stumbled upon his mate in the middle of a fucking mission. He couldn't have prepared for this.

After a long, tense moment, the woman took a deep breath and lifted her chin, almost challenging him. Bez's wolf perked up, eyeing her, waiting to see what she had planned. She gave Bez a hard look, one that made his wolf whine inside his head. One that made his blood rush south to his long-neglected cock.

"I need to take a shower," she said, her voice firm.

Bez felt his eyebrows draw together. He wanted to ask her what he'd done wrong and how to fix it, but he stayed silent. Instead, he pointed toward the back of the house. The woman nodded once, glanced at the wolf at his side, and strode down the hall toward the bathroom. He watched her go, a sense of dread knotting his gut and telling him he'd just made a huge mistake. Not a familiar feeling for him.

The wolf at his side, the Omega named Angelita, whined as she watched her friend leave.

"She wants to bathe," Bez said, frowning at how unnecessary the words were. "I have no idea what just happened."

Angelita chuffed, an almost mocking sound, which seemed fitting considering the situation.

"What?" Bez asked. "Am I supposed to know what's going on in that woman's head?"

Angelita didn't answer. Instead, the wolf hopped on the couch and waited, watching him, making Bez feel somehow expected to do...something. When he didn't move, she barked. Bez growled in response, his own wolf forcing his human spirit aside. The shewolf wagged her tail and perked her ears as she waited, the picture of youthful ignorance. If she knew the kind of man he was, the things he'd done over the years, she wouldn't want him anywhere near her. But right then, she did.

Bez approached the couch with caution, his steps slow. He wasn't afraid of the little wolf, but she made him feel off-balance, just as his mate did. That sensation was something he didn't like, something he was unaccustomed to experiencing. He recognized that he was treating the women as if they were dangerous, and wasn't that just a mind fuck. A tiny teenage shewolf and his own mate, dangerous to *him*.

With more care than probably necessary considering the small build of the girl, Bez lowered himself to the couch, leaving lots of space between him and Angelita. She shuffled closer, making soft, chuffing noises. Bez growled back, his wolf uncertain if her actions were some kind of challenge or not.

When her nose hit his thigh, Bez huffed. "If you have something to say, Omega, shift back and say it."

The wolf froze, staring at him deep and hard for a moment before she dropped her eyes. Bez could almost feel the sadness pouring off her, the desperation. His wolf surged forward, seeing her as something to guard and protect. More so than just in the context of following Blaze's orders. He suddenly saw her as pack, which threw Bez even more off-balance. He wasn't a protector. He was a hunter, a tracker, and an assassin. His idea of keeping the Omega safe had been to lock her in the safe room and wait until someone else could deal with her. Now he had two Omegas on his hands, and he couldn't imagine leaving either of them alone.

Unsure what to do next, Bez said the only words he could think of. "You can't shift back, can you?"

Angelita shook her head and whimpered.

"I've never tried to reverse a forced shift, but we could try. If you wanted to." He held up his hands at her fierce growl. "No. Okay. Gotcha."

The red wolf relaxed again, though her eyes were still wary and watchful. Untrusting. Regret wasn't something Bez was used to bearing, but he practically bowed under the weight of it right then. Regret for not protecting her better, regret for forcing her to shift, regret for not knowing how to fix what he'd done.

He didn't like this regret shit.

Bez lifted his hand, his movements unsteady and awkward. Compassion wasn't his thing... He didn't touch. He didn't feel. He didn't... Without allowing himself time to think his actions through, he brought his hand around to the back of Angelita's neck. And he rubbed.

"It's okay," he said, staring at the way his fingers moved in her fur. Wondering when the last time he'd voluntarily touched someone other than in a formal greeting had been. "Those first shifts can be brutal. I couldn't shift at will until I was nineteen. Before that, every shift my father forced upon me was painful and seemed to take forever, and coming back on my own was such a long and arduous process."

The girl watched him with her wide eyes. Waiting for something he couldn't identify. Bez's massage faltered, his mouth going dry. Fuck, what was he supposed to say? The Omega lay there looking at him, not giving him any clue as to what she wanted. Bez hated not knowing the next step in a plan. Hated it so much, he refused to live that way. But damn, the two Omegas had thrown his world completely upside down in the course of just one evening. And the night wasn't over yet.

Sighing, rubbing his free hand over his head, he surrendered to those deep, dark eyes staring up at him. "You'll shift back when you're ready. You're still too young yet to deal with the pressure I put on you. I… shouldn't have forced you to shift that way."

As Bez fell silent, he found himself staring down the hall where his mate had disappeared. Angelita must have felt more comfortable with his silence than his words. She inched closer, curling up next to him with her head on his knee. Bez kept his fingers buried in her fur, the close proximity of another shifter calming the confusion in his mind. A very unexpected benefit of the whole touching thing. The comfort soothed him, lulled him into a state of emotion he'd never experienced.

"Did I mess something up?" The words almost surprised him, the weakness behind them something he hadn't wanted to share.

Angelita sniffed, an agreeable sound if he had to guess.

Bez swallowed, listening to the sounds coming from down the hall. The water falling and meeting skin, the splash of something against tile. The noises that came from his mate as she bathed.

His *mate*...

"I don't know how to do this." Bez licked his lips, fighting to get the words out. "I've never done anything like this. Ever. She's..."

He couldn't say it, couldn't tell Angelita he'd found his mate before he said the words to the woman herself. A woman whose name he didn't yet know.

"Oh, shit." Bez rubbed a rough hand over his shorn head. He hadn't asked her name, and he certainly hadn't offered his. True, he'd made sure to save her along with Angelita, purely for selfish reasons if he were being honest, but he hadn't treated her as a mate should be treated. He hadn't made things easier on her or offered her a single piece of himself. He hadn't even told her *his name*.

But the danger hadn't subsided, and he was still thinking like a soldier, not a mate. The threat of a hunting werewolf during a full moon was a real one, particularly for the women. The men from the camp would find them, dragging the beast along with them. They'd try to control it, to keep it away from the Omega and send it after his mate. A woman they saw as disposable. That thought made his blood boil and his wolf snarl viciously in his head. His mate was no more disposable than he was, and he'd prove it to anyone who dared treat her otherwise. But he'd need help to eliminate the threat.

"Fuck." Bez threw his head back and pulled his phone from the pocket of his shorts. He'd never made this kind of call, never had to ask for help from anyone outside of his brothers. Not until now. Not until he started working outside of his orders.

His fingers flew over the screen as he dialed the number from memory. Carefully, he lifted Angelita's muzzle off his thigh, letting it fall back to the seat of the couch as he stood up. Bez stalked across the floor as he waited for Dante to pick up, growling low and steady. This had to work. There was nothing more he could do, not on his own. He had a job to do in keeping Angelita safe from harm, but he had a personal responsibility to his mate as well. Both women were his to care for, and he couldn't do it alone. He needed help to keep both women safe.

After what seemed like a hundred rings, Dante's voice came through the other end. "What's the news, Bez?"

"Change in plans."

Dante's pause would have been almost unnoticeable to anyone else, but Bez had worked closely with him and Blaze for a long time. That pause might as well have been a scream.

"What's the situation?" Dante asked, his voice a bit lower.

"Three shifters heading our way, plus a werewolf on the hunt."

"Ah, fuck." The click of Dante's typing sounded like automatic gunfire in the distance, his fingers obviously flying fast over the keys. "How much time?"

"Couple of hours at most."

"Damn it, Beelzebub. You're not giving us a lot of options."

Bez squeezed his eyes shut. "I know, sir."

"You have a place to hole up?"

"The lake house outside of Port Barre. There's an arsenal and a safe room. I hate to use it, but it'll work to keep the were away from—" Bez took a deep breath "—the Omegas."

The silence on the other end lasted far longer than Dante's original pause, not something anyone would miss. Bez knew the information that there were two Omegas involved would shock the shifter.

After almost twenty seconds of stunned silence, Dante growled, "What do you mean, Omegas? Please tell me you misspoke."

Bez made another pass around the room, slowing slightly. "There were two Omegas at the camp, sir."

Dante cursed low and guttural. "And you took them both with you?"

"Yes, sir."

More silence. Bez's head shot up as the shower turned off, his ears perking at the scratch of a towel against skin. His mate would be finished soon, and he still had no idea what to say to her.

Angelita hopped off the couch and walked down the hall, leaving Bez to his phone call. He listened as she trotted into the back right bedroom and jumped on the bed, the mattress creaking under even her slight weight. He'd need to move her upstairs soon, into the cold, steel box that could keep her alive in the event the were got past him, but he could allow her to sleep downstairs in a comfortable bed for now. If he kept his wolf closer to the surface, he'd hear the threat of the men and their beast coming long before they hit the property.

"Do we know which pack Omega Two belongs to?" Dante asked, drawing Bez's attention back to the conversation.

"No, sir."

"Does she match the descriptions of any of the missing Omegas reported?"

"No, sir."

"Have you questioned her?"

"No, sir."

"How do you know she's not a threat?"

Bez paused, listening as his mate padded across the tile floor of the bathroom. The soldier in him said to give Dante all the details, to tell him he'd found his mate in the second Omega. But again, Bez didn't want to say the words for the first time unless they were to *her*. Something in him, some deep and nearly dead place inside, told him that was the right thing to do. To tell others instead first would be disrespectful to her and to the sanctity of the mating claim. And if there was one thing a Dire Wolf understood, it was the importance of respect.

So Bez took a breath, he focused on the sound of the woman who'd just opened the bathroom door, and he withheld information from Dante for the first time since they'd started working together.

"I just do, sir."

Thirteen

ariel stayed under the pulsing heat of the shower for as long as she dared, letting the hot water wash away the filth that covered her body. If only there were a way to wash away the bad memories as well. For two months, she'd been kept captive in that hell of a houseboat, half of the time alone and terrified. Hell, if she were completely honest, she'd spent every damned second terrified. And though she wanted to believe that part of her life was over, she doubted. Those men were still out there, coming for her and Angelita. The only thing standing in the way being her mate.

Her mate... *ugh*.

The shower may have left her feeling refreshed, but it did little to soothe her splintered ego. Her mate was not good with words, that much was blatantly obvious. When he said she wasn't part of the plan, Sariel thought her heart would break. The gut-wrenching fear of him regretting bringing her with him had consumed her. But as the water swirling down the drain went from black to gray to clear, so did those thoughts and insecurities. No matter how little they knew each other, they were now tied in a way most shifters dreamed about. She needed to pull up her big-girl panties, nonexistent as they were at the moment, and face down the beast so she could find out where she stood.

She was going to have to actually speak to her mate about more than just how to stay alive.

"It's just talking," Sariel whispered into the spray, letting the water drown her words. Stomach rolling at the thought of how badly this could go, she reluctantly turned off the taps. A chill set in fast, her body overheated from the shower, but she didn't move. Instead, she stood with her hands braced on the tile wall, not ready to leave the safety of the steamy bathroom.

Finally, Sariel huffed and dragged open the glass door. She couldn't hide forever. She dried off quickly and threw on the T-shirt she'd acquired in the Jeep, unable not to notice the little round hole sitting almost exactly at the top of her hip. A perfect circle, darkened around the edges. So very odd if only in its simplicity. She stuck her finger through the hole and wiggled it, contemplating why the man would keep a shirt with a hole in it. Sentimental reasons? He didn't seem much like the sentimental sort, but it was always a possibility. Some kind of memory tied to it? Good or bad, that might be a reason to keep it. Or was he simply someone who refused to give up on things, who saw the flaws as minor?

Sariel sighed. She was putting way too much thought into a simple T-shirt with a hole in it. She needed to quit stalling. After one more moment staring at the damned hole, she tossed her head back and looked at herself in the steamy mirror.

"Time to put your game face on." She took two deep breaths and squared her shoulders, readying herself to confront the man the fates deemed hers. She needed to know where she stood with him and if he even had any interest in being mated. Some men didn't. It was rare to be outright rejected, but the possibility existed. She'd just have to ask him…be blunt and direct. And she would. As soon as she could breathe properly while thinking about him rejecting her.

Ready to escape the steamy bathroom but still afraid to talk to her mate, Sariel opened the door and followed Angelita's scent to the bedroom on the right. She found the red wolf on one of the twin-size beds, curled into a furry ball. The girl slept soundly with no sign of tears on the fur of her muzzle. Finally. Sariel wished she could join her on the other fluffy bed, snuggle under real blankets and curl up around an actual pillow, but she needed to settle things first. Before she lost her nerve.

Sariel closed her eyes and sent a wish up to the fates before heading down the hallway toward the living room. Every step seemed to take less time than the last as her blood rushed in a roar through her ears. She wanted the hall to never end, yet it seemed to disappear right in front of her eyes.

She turned the corner to find the man who had been owning her thoughts since she first saw him, sitting by the fireplace. His big body leaned forward in his chair as he stared at the exact spot where she'd appeared. As if waiting for her, knowing she was coming for him. His eyes were dark, his face hard, causing her to falter in her step. He was not a man to be messed with on a good day, and if his expression was any indication, this was not a good day.

His eyes dropped to the hem of the T-shirt she wore. His shirt. Her fingers followed his gaze, worrying the edges of the fabric. Suddenly walking around without anything underneath the dark cotton seemed like a mistake. Wearing no underwear or pants left her feeling vulnerable and exposed. At risk. And yet something in his expression made her body tingle, made the arousal his nearness incited flare up bright and powerful.

Heart racing, breaths coming faster, skin flushed hot, she stood and waited to see which way this would go. Accepted or refused, mated or rejected. Claimed or scared away. And she was scared, at least a little bit. The danger in his body language made her both anxious and turned on in equal measure, teasing and tormenting her in cruel and lovely ways. Not something she'd ever experienced before.

Her fingers ran along the soft fabric as she wished the shirt were both shorter and longer at the same time. He tracked the movement like a hunter eyeing its prey. Like a starving man being teased with a juicy steak. She wondered what it would be like to be his steak.

His eyes slid along the planes of her body, over her breasts and neck, his head angling a bit to one side as he watched her. Investigated her. Learned every curve and dip.

"You have freckles," he whispered, his voice rough but soft.

"Oh…" Sariel froze, her plans for demanding he talk to her blown up by the simple fact that he *had* talked to her, especially about the freckles that covered most of her body. "I…yeah. Always have."

He sat silent for a moment, his eyes dropping to her hips as she took two small steps closer. God, she could practically feel him touching her with that predatory gaze. So dark…so intense. A physical force in just a look.

"I'm Bez." He slid his teeth over his bottom lip, his canines long and sharp. Deadly weapons against soft, pink flesh. Dangerous and sexy all at once. Just like everything else about him.

Sariel shivered and took another step. "Bez?"

He froze her with a glance, his eyes swirling from ice to silver as he clenched his jaw. "It's short...for Beelzebub. The name my pack assigned me."

She nodded as she inched closer, her footsteps light and slow. "But people call you Bez."

"Mostly."

Sariel stopped when her knees brushed his, her entire body burning hot at his nearness. "May I call you Bez?"

He tipped his head back and let his knees fall open as he watched her. Examined her. Absorbed her. "If that pleases you."

She inched between his legs, growing more confident with every word he uttered. Every lengthy look. His fingers brushed against her thigh, his skin warm and rough as it whispered against hers. She shivered and moved closer. His eyes dropped to her hip, a frown pulling at his mouth. He reached out, using one finger to trace around the edge of the hole at her hip, his brow furrowed.

"I..." Bez said, shaking his head. "I wish I had better."

Sariel smiled, placing her hand over his, stilling his finger as she pressed his hand flat against her hip. "It's fine. I don't need much."

"What you need and what you deserve are two

different things, Freckles."

She liked that statement, liked the way the warmth in his voice caressed her. She liked that a lot. She slowly dropped her weight onto his thigh, demanding more contact, teasing the beast. And he was a beast; a strong and fierce wolf shifter fully in tune with his inner animal. More soldier than man, more wolf than anything, he was one tightly wound ball of instinct and aggression.

She wanted to unravel him.

"I like the way Bez feels on my lips," she whispered. He blinked but otherwise didn't respond. He also didn't try to pull her any closer or touch her in any way. Not making a move, but not pushing her away either. A challenge of sorts, one she was more than ready for. "My name's Sariel."

Bez nodded once, his eyes staying on hers. "We didn't know about you."

She sighed, a pang in her heart reminding her of the home she'd been stolen from. "My pack is small and stuck in their ways. They're not part of the NALB, and I doubt they would've reported anything even if they were."

Sariel grew quiet, worrying her lip as she perched on his leg. She began to feel quite silly for sitting on him, but his presence brought her peace. His touch soothed her wolf in a way she needed desperately after so long locked up in that hell of a houseboat. Still, when it became obvious Bez wasn't going to speak on his own, she took a deep breath.

"Can we...talk?" she whispered, her voice almost weak.

Bez grunted and looked away, his jaw clenched and the muscles in his neck stiff. Sariel's heart sank. That certainly seemed to answer her question on how he felt about being mated. She moved to stand up, but Bez's hand tightened on her hip, holding her in place.

"Don't," he said. "Don't stop...touching."

Sariel peered into his eyes. The cold blue gave nothing away. "You want me to touch you?"

Bez paused then nodded. "I just... I don't normally do this."

"What? Touching?" Sariel gave him a soft smile when he nodded. "You can, you know. Touch me. I don't mind."

He growled and turned away again, but then his fingertips brushed her thigh. A tiny brush of his flesh that meant more than a full hug would have. Sariel waited, barely breathing, as she watched his hand creep along her leg, fingers twitching along the way.

"I don't know how to do this," he whispered, keeping his eyes on his fingers.

"Yes, you do." Sariel brought her hand to his chest, laying her palm over his pounding heart. "I think you know how to touch just fine."

"Not that." He raised his eyes to hers, his expression

practically stabbing her in the heart. "This."

Sariel waited for more, but it never came. Still, she felt his need for her touch, felt how much he wanted her to stay close. There was a deep craving within him for physical contact, though he seemed too scared or stunted to express it. But she saw. She knew. She understood him in a way that took her by surprise.

"Do you mean being mated?" she asked. "Because I don't know how to do that either, though I'm not opposed to the idea."

Bez's eyes went wide. Sariel wondered if that was the first time he'd been so obviously caught off guard.

She leaned forward once more, keeping her voice soft as she asked, "Do you want to be mated?"

Bez nodded, all slow and intentional. Sariel bit her lip and took a deep breath, bold under his touch.

"Do you want to be mated to me?"

He growled, low and deep. A dark sound that made her lick her lips and shift closer on his leg. Sexy…he was just so damn sexy.

"Freckles." Bez pushed her hair over her shoulder, his fingers gentle and slow. "I've been alone a long time. I don't know how to do all the talking stuff."

"You seem to be doing fine."

He shook his head and looked away, though his hand crept up along her waist to cup her hip, pulling her closer. Breathing hard, Sariel leaned in, dropping her head until she brushed her nose against his.

"Maybe we don't need to talk." She eyed his mouth, wanting to kiss him, needing to feel his lips on hers. His eyes stayed open, watching her. His body tense and hard. Sariel leaned closer, pressing her breasts against his chest, breathing in his breath when he spoke. "Maybe we can just…feel."

Bez's growl turned rougher, deeper, vibrating against her skin in a way that was both warning and enticement.

"My kind," he said, his voice barely more than a whisper. "We're not…gentle."

That voice, so low and sultry as he cautioned her against him. It made her blood positively boil inside of her. Made her crave him—his touch, his taste, his smell. She wanted him. Hell, she burned for him.

"I don't need gentle." Sariel nodded her consent, a slow and sensual move that made her nose run along his. He brought a hand to her face, cupped her cheek, and ran his thumb over her bottom lip. Soft… maddeningly soft.

"Beautiful," he whispered just as his lips brushed hers. Sariel closed her eyes and let herself experience this first kiss, let herself truly feel him. The way his lips pursed into hers, how his fingers tightened almost unconsciously on her hip, the brush of his knuckles as he dropped his hand from her face to grip the back of her neck. The way he held her. Owning her. Possessing her with a single kiss.

She moaned and opened her mouth, desperate to taste him. Needing him inside of her in some way. Bez answered her invitation, sliding his tongue into her mouth, groaning his satisfaction. Sariel lived in that kiss, let his tongue dominate hers. She gave without taking until he withdrew. And then she bit his bottom lip...hard.

With a growl, Bez pulled her closer, directing her legs on either side of his. Sariel slid her hips forward, straddling him, wishing to everything that the fabric between them could magically disappear. Wanting his flesh on hers, to feel every inch of him.

Rocking her hips, sliding along the length of where he was obviously hard for her, she kissed and nipped at his lips. He did the same, his touch demanding. His kiss near painful. His growls turned deeper, the sound vibrating through his body and into hers. She liked it, liked the way his rough hands and strong lips made her feel: safe, cared for, protected. Desired.

He gripped her hips harder, pressing her down on his lap. He was so hard. So thick and hot even through the shorts he wore. Sariel wrapped her arms around his neck and rolled her hips over the length of him, but a roar from outside stopped her midstroke. She gasped and jerked back, clinging to Bez as her heart nearly exploded. He jumped to his feet, hooking an arm around her waist and bringing her with him, lifting her with ease. He snarled as he turned toward the noise, twisting his body to keep Sariel behind him, his growl fierce and vicious.

"It's a gator," she said, rubbing his muscled arm even as her own heart thundered in her chest. "The sound scared me, but it's nothing. They make noises like that all the time."

Bez's hand on Sariel's hip moved down, his grip lessening. "They scare you."

Sariel tightened her hold on his shirt and rested her forehead against his back. His words weren't a question, they were a statement. An observation. A truth.

"Yes."

"They won't hurt you." Bez released her hip and turned, his eyes nearly glowing in the low light. "I won't let them."

Sariel's heart stuttered and her face heated under his stare. God, the man made her crazy…in good and bad ways.

"I know."

Bez ran a hand over his face and sighed, his shoulders stiff. "You should get some rest."

Sariel nodded. "Yeah…okay."

She turned, but Bez's hand gripped her elbow, stopping her. He pulled her back against his body, wrapping one arm around her hips and holding her tight.

"I need to listen for them," he whispered before leaning down to place a kiss on her forehead. "I can't concentrate with you so close, and I can't let them surprise me."

Sariel nodded, curling into the warmth of his body, sighing when his arm tightened and pulled her even closer. "You think they're coming tonight?"

"I know they are. It's just a matter of when."

"And you have people coming to help?"

"Yeah. But they're a ways out."

"So we wait to see who gets here first."

Bez looked down at her, his face serious, his eyes quicksilver light. "I won't let them touch you. Either of you."

Sariel ran her hand along his jaw and smiled. "I know."

He leaned down, rubbing his nose against hers before trailing his lips over her cheek and jaw to her neck. Breathing her in. Scenting her.

"You took me by surprise," he whispered, his breath tickling her neck. "I'm not a man who's surprised often." He placed a single, small kiss to her neck then let her go. "You should head back with Angelita and rest while you can."

Sariel sighed and pulled out of his arms reluctantly. She hated walking away from him, but she was tired from a long night of running, escaping, worrying, and dealing with her mate. Even just a nap would be helpful. Besides, danger was on its way and she'd need to be extra awake and aware when they arrived. Especially if she was going to be any help for Bez.

When Sariel reached the hallway, she paused and turned, watching as Bez settled into his chair once more. "What about you?"

Bez cocked his head. "What about me?"

"Don't you need to rest?"

"No, I'm fine. I'd rather see you get some sleep."

Sariel nodded and moved down the hall, tossing back over her shoulder, "You're better at this being mated stuff than you realize, Bez."

He smiled, the first time she'd seen his lips turn up like that, and it warmed her heart to no end. "Good to know, Freckles."

Fourteen

Soft hips and thighs teased Bez as he watched his mate disappear down the hall. Just the thought of those dark eyes looking up at him, those sultry lips all swollen and wet from his kiss made him nearly insane with a possessive lust that surprised him. And the freckles…good goddamn. Like some kind of primal mating pattern stamped right into her skin. They called to him, made his fingers itch to touch her, stirred up something dirty deep inside of him. He hadn't known freckles could be so sexy.

His mate pulled feelings from him he'd never experienced; never even known he was capable of. For centuries, he'd lived with his pack of Dire Wolves, hunting beasts great and small, traveling where others asked him to go. In defense of the Omegas, the lost Dire

Wolf females, he'd become a soldier for hire, sticking close to whoever had the most power and could enable him and his pack to protect the shewolves. He'd never broken rank, gone against orders, or failed at a mission. Hell, he'd never even paused to accept a challenge thrown his way, no matter how dangerous. He'd fought werewolves, almost died from a vampire attack, and killed off more shifters than he could count…all in the name of the mission.

But suddenly, after nothing more than a look from Sariel, he no longer knew what to do next. By not telling Dante about their connection, he was technically going rogue. And though his pack would probably understand his hesitancy, he wondered if his actions would be seen as a weakness.

For the first time in his life, he felt the need to ease up on his Dire Wolf responsibilities. After this mission, he wasn't sure if he wanted to continue hunting down criminals with the rest of his pack or if he wanted to take a break. Spend some time getting to know his mate. Maybe take her home with him and show her how much he'd prepared for this day. Because he had prepared, even if he hadn't meant to. He had a den ready and waiting for them. He had trinkets and treasures from all over the world. Things he'd hoarded without knowing exactly why. His property was situated in the perfect spot to keep her safe, to protect her.

And protect her he would. At all costs.

The sudden silence outside caught his attention, the odd break in background noise slamming into Bez's thoughts, pulling him from dreaming about his new mate. He stretched his senses, letting his wolf push forward. His ears rose and pricked, his mouth lengthened—half man, half wolf, he gave himself over to hearing and scent. Miles out yet, the sound of paws meeting earth whispered through the night. A pack was coming...moving closer. A quick glance at the clock had Bez slamming back to his human form and uttering a curse as he exploded to his feet. It was too early for his team to have reached the area, not to mention his guys would never have made enough noise to be heard from so far away. No, those heavy pawfalls had to be the kidnappers coming to take back the Omegas. To take Bez's mate from him. The very thought had him moving faster and fighting back a warning roar. Those fuckers wouldn't get near his Sariel. His mission was to save the Omega, and though he knew Blaze had meant Angelita, his mate was an Omega just the same. He would do whatever it took to keep them both safe.

Never had a mission been so personal; never had getting it right been so vital.

With little more than a flick of his wrist, he pulled his phone from his pocket and speed-dialed Levi. When his brother answered, the music blasting in the background told Bez he was already on the road.

"Status."

Bez glanced out a window before checking the lock. "Situation FUBAR. Get your ass here."

"Roger. Currently a little less than three hours out."

Bez growled, moving from window to window and verifying the house was ready. "Not good enough. I've got less than an hour."

"Fuck," Levi hissed. The engine noise grew in the background, the shifter obviously pushing the engine harder. "You're too far out for any of us to meet that time, man."

"I know." Bez took a deep breath as he checked the last door, dread heavy in his gut. "Just haul ass."

"Hauling. The cavalry will get there."

Bez hung up without another word, knowing there was nothing left to say. The cavalry would arrive eventually, but not nearly soon enough. He was on his own for this attack.

Rushing toward the back of the house, Bez zeroed in on the steady heartbeats of the women. They slept apart, one in each of the two bedrooms at the rear of the house, which worked to his advantage. Access to the attic safe room was in the hallway just outside their doors. He had a good forty minutes or so before the shifters made it to the property if their trajectory and pace stayed the same, but he didn't want to take any chances. The sooner he got both women to safety, the better.

Bez slipped into the bedroom where Sariel slept,

his attention divided between his mate and the men running closer outside. The woman was curled up on one side of the huge bed, buried under fluffy white blankets. Calm, resting, and quiet. And by the gods, was that a welcoming sight. His mate could have gone into the other bedroom, the one where Angelita slept. There were two beds in there. But no, she'd chosen the larger room—the one with a single, huge bed. A bed made for a couple.

A bed made for sex.

Focus. He had to fucking focus. The pack hadn't changed speed; they were still far enough away for him to get the women into the safe room and work out a plan so long as he stopped thinking with his dick.

Bez hurried to Sariel's bed. He needed her awake but calm. This wasn't the time to scare her like he had at the houseboat. He leaned low over his mate's body, barely inches away, placing a knee on the edge of the bed to move closer. He peeled back the blankets over her, whimpering at the sight of her nearly naked body. Damn, she smelled good, all sweet and sexy and his. Still wearing his T-shirt, which had been hiked up to reveal the delicious curves of her ass, she slept on her side facing the door. Bez wanted to run a finger down her cheek or wake her with soft kisses to her neck, but the threat loomed large in the woods, and time was not his friend.

Silently apologizing for his actions, he leaned close

to Sariel and clamped his hand over her mouth. He'd expected her to react with fear. To jump, to scream, to fight back against some unknown attacker. Instead, she growled soft and purrlike as she grabbed him by the arms and pulled him down on top of her. Bez fell easily, partly because of his unbalanced stance and partly because it was his mate pulling him into bed with her. Of course, he'd fall.

Without opening her eyes, Sariel wrapped her legs around Bez's hips and melted against him. Bez tried to resist, to pull away, but she was so warm, so soft, and so his. He tucked his face into her neck, scenting her, unable to hold back his growl. Her heat was a delicious tease, her body soft beneath his. Pliant. Willing and wanting at the same time. And he wanted, too. He wanted so fucking bad.

He rocked his hips against hers, slipping into the cradle of her thighs. Desperate to get closer. He held himself back, though, not wanting to push her too far. He didn't even think she'd woken up all the way yet; he couldn't just rut her through the mattress. But then her eyes opened, heavy-lidded and sleepy but open. And she gave him the most brilliant, sexy smile.

Aw, fuck.

Sariel slid her hands around his neck, holding him tightly as she sighed and shifted her hips back and forth. Bez tried to resist, to keep himself from losing his focus and giving in to the mating haze, but Sariel was a warrior against his control. She yanked him down on top of her, fighting to bring him closer. She wiggled and stretched until she'd pushed his shorts down and off his legs using nothing but her feet. Talented little mate. When she'd freed him from the fabric that was apparently in her way, she wrapped her legs around his waist again. Aligning them with every lift and buck of her hips. Driving him fucking mad with desire. She battled hard, his little mate, and even against his best judgment, he surrendered to her.

Without a single word, he pressed into the swollen heat of her pussy and wrapped his arms around her. Pulling her tightly and caging her against his body. She growled and rocked until she had him seated deep inside her, until she groaned and shivered with every single thrust. Bodies moving together, no space between them, hushed grunts and groans and gasps the only break in the silence around them. The sounds destroyed him, had his body rushing for a climax he desperately wanted to hold off on. Just a few minutes, even.

Bez closed his eyes, losing all sense of time and place as Sariel took him in, rocking her hips with his and squeezing his cock in the best possible way. So hot, so soft. And so very, very naked underneath that T-shirt. He wanted to rip it from her body, reveal every inch of her to him. The fabric had ridden up to her chest, the bottom curves of her breasts teasing him whenever he pulled back enough to look down. He wanted to see her dark nipples again, to fulfill the deep desire to touch and taste and bite the sight of them had caused when they were in the swamp. But those tantalizing circles were still hidden, still covered by his gray T-shirt, and as hard as it was to resist tearing it off her, the waiting for the shirt to rise on its own was the best tease he'd ever experienced.

"Bez," Sariel whispered, bucking harder and clutching at the back of his neck. Bez took that as a signal she was close, collapsing on her with all his weight and thrusting harder. Plunging deep and holding there as he rocked his hips against hers. As he pressed against her sweet pussy, dying to pay her clit a little extra attention.

Her lips found the curve where his neck met his shoulder, following the kiss with a gentle bite. Bez shivered at the feel of her teeth against him and fought back a possessive growl. Damn it, they weren't alone and had a pack of shifters closing in on them, but he couldn't stop. The instinct to mate and mark and claim was nearly impossible to resist. He needed to pull away, to stop fucking her and to keep his dick to himself, but good God, it felt so amazing. So right. Hips rocking, flexing his back to hit the exact spots that would make Sariel shiver and sigh, he bit his lip and counted down. Thirty more seconds. He could give her that long, and then he'd have to yank himself free of the urge to mate and get her moving toward the attic. He just had to make her come in thirty seconds.

Bez slipped his hand between them, brushing his knuckle against the soft flesh of her pussy. Wet and hot and so much his. She sighed and shivered again, spreading her legs for him. Rushing him. He wanted to take his time, to explore more, but that would have to wait for next time. For the thousands of next times he'd make sure they'd have together.

He worked his finger against her clit, circling and pressing harder on each pass as she gasped and arched into his touch. Hands clutching at him, breasts pressed tightly against his chest, his name on her lips… She was close. She was also undeniably sexy. And his. All his.

"Mine." His growl came as a surprise, but it had the best effect on Sariel. She bit her lip to hold back her cry and arched her back, finally letting go. Her pussy tightened around him, so hard and strong, he felt every pulse. The pressure caused him to come with a jolt, the two of them joined in their pleasure. Still rocking, still rubbing that little clit, still trying to give her as much as he could.

When she finally relaxed, finally sagged into the plush pillows, she opened those beautiful eyes of hers again, and she smiled.

"I wasn't expecting that."

Bez sighed, sliding out of her as he leaned to kiss the tip of her nose. "Neither was I. You're quite demanding in your sleep."

She giggled softly, rubbing her hands up and down his back. He wanted to fall onto the mattress next to her, to snuggle close and wrap his body around hers in protection. But he couldn't. Danger was coming.

"We didn't kiss," she whispered, words that pulled Bez up short.

"What?"

"Well, we had…sex. But we didn't kiss."

Bez blinked, his brow pulling tight. How could he explain his life to her in the few seconds he had?

"I've never kissed a partner during sex."

It was Sariel's turn to blink as she stared. "You've never kissed…what?"

He leaned down, running his nose along the length of hers as he whispered, "I've never kissed another person at all, Sariel. You were my first kiss tonight."

"Oh." Her whispered exclamation was followed by her soft, pink tongue licking her bottom lip. Just the tip, a tiny swipe, but Bez became obsessed with it. Wanted to feel the softness against his own. Everything about her seemed soft. He liked that, liked the way she felt in his hands.

Sariel nudged her chin upward, parting her lips just a bit, and closed her eyes. Bez kept his open, kept watching her as he dropped a little lower with each breath. His first kiss had been with this woman, but it hadn't been planned. This felt more important, somehow. More vital to the two of them as a mated pair. Such a ridiculous thing, kissing, and yet he was completely on edge.

Sariel was the brave one of the two, closing the distance between them and pressing her lips to his. He growled low and deep, shivering as her tongue swiped across his lip. Fuck, this was so much hotter than he'd ever thought. Naked, lying in a bed beside a woman, and kissing her. But it was more than just some woman. This was his mate, and he knew nothing could compare to the feelings she pulled from him. A simple brush of his mate's lips, and he was hard again. Ready for more, needing to bury himself in her. Fully ensconced in the mating haze.

But then she opened her mouth a bit more, and her tongue entered his. Tangled with his own. And he fucking died. Or at least, his focus did. He grabbed her against him, rolling them to the side as he kissed her with as much force as he dared. She responded to his efforts, the two sliding tongues together in a way that was more like fucking than Bez had ever imagined. In and out, hot and wet. So much pressure and desire, so much lust. So much better than even their first kiss.

Sariel had just pulled back to nip his bottom lip, had just blessed him with the feeling of her teeth on his flesh and made his cock practically weep in anticipation, when Bez heard the crashing of the wolves through the woods on two sides of the property. The sound was enough to pull him free of the imperative to claim his mate, to drag him out of his lust-filled haze and set him back on task. Cursing, he bit her lip and gave her a last soft kiss. They were out of time.

Bez sat up with a sigh, his heart breaking at the look of disappointment in her eyes. "You have to go."

Sariel gasped, clinging to the sheet and pulling it up against her chest, looking slightly heartbroken. Shit, again with the messing up. Bez's heart stuttered at the pained expression on her face, and he quickly grabbed her arm and pulled her closer.

"No, Freckles." Bez shook his head. "You have to go up to the safe room. They're here."

It took a moment for the words to register, but when they did, she practically exploded off the bed. Her feet barely making a sound, she hurried to Angelita's room without a look back, waking the wolf with soft whispers. Bez yanked on his shorts and followed her into the hall, listening hard to the noises the pack outside was making.

Once the red wolf awoke, Sariel looked back his way, her eyes wide and filled with a fear that made his soul ache. "Are you sure it's not your team?"

Bez watched her, trying to keep his words smooth and steady so as not to scare either of the two Omegas under his protection. "No, not yet. Soon, but it's time to get you both into the safe room."

Sariel nodded, something Bez took to mean she

understood. Which was good because, by the way the sounds outside were growing closer, they only had a handful of minutes until the first wolf would be at their door.

Bez hurried Sariel and Angelita into the hallway, sliding open the attic access panel and pulling the ladder down with ease.

"Up we go." Bez grabbed Angelita and brought her to his chest before giving Sariel a look he hoped said more than his words could in that moment. Words like *I'm sorry, I want to get to know you, you're my mate, and I need you safe.* All things he didn't have time for, so he said what he could with his eyes as he whispered, "After you."

Bez followed his mate up the ladder, staying close to her. Close enough for his arms to rub against her ass with every move as he hurried her up the steps while carrying Angelita. Her very naked ass, he noticed repeatedly. He needed to find her something to wear, but there wasn't enough time. Not with the enemy so close.

Once Bez's feet hit the attic floor, he led the girls to the safe room door. After he entered the code and released the latch, he swung open the heavy door and set Angelita down just over the threshold.

"It's steel; they can't get through," he whispered, purposely keeping his voice low as the wolves outside came closer. Sariel stared up at him, all breathless and flushed. Kissable. Fuckable. But not then. "Get in and lock the door. I'll be back when this is over."

"What about you?" Sariel asked, fear showing in her gaze. She grabbed his wrist, her fingers soft and hot against his skin. That touch set him on fire, making him growl his want for her. Bez couldn't hold back. He picked her up and crashed his lips to hers, kissing her with all the need and desire he had for her. She met his kiss with the same fervor, not backing down, owning him as much as he was trying to own her.

His hands gripped her ass, pulling her tight, squeezing her closer. Keeping his body against his for one glorious moment. But the enemy was too close, and Bez needed to get his mind back in the fight. After one final lip bite that made Sariel sigh, he pulled back, knowing his time was up as the first footfall fell on the grass of the lawn.

"Gotta go."

Sariel stepped into the safe room, her chin up and her eyes dry. His brave little mate putting on a show for him and Angelita. "Be careful."

"Stay put." Bez pushed the door closed, resting his hands against the cool steel for a moment longer than necessary before whispering, "Be safe."

As soon as Bez heard the click of the lock engaging, he stalked across the attic and slid down the ladder. With a single push, he slid the access panel back into place, making the entrance almost invisible. He would have liked to have hidden their scent trail as well, but it was too late. The wolves were on the property, though there was still no scent or sound of the werewolf. That worried him more than if the beast had been on the porch or breaking through the windows. Its absence told him the jackasses had a plan and a strategy. Too bad Bez did as well, one that would decimate theirs. Lights off, house silent, Bez smiled and gave himself over to his inner wolf.

It was time to fight for the Omegas…time to kill for his mate's safety.

Fifteen

"Be careful," Sariel said, her heart in her throat.

Fear wrapped around her like a vise, strangling her voice. She gave herself one more moment to look over her mate—her strong, capable, warrior mate—before she pulled the heavy door closed. The lock dropped into place with a clank, the sound ominous in the hollow space. She leaned her forehead against the steel panel and closed her eyes.

"Be safe," Bez said from behind the door, and then nothing. Silence.

A whine from behind her made Sariel open her eyes, fighting back the burn of unshed tears. Forcing the worry from her heart, she turned toward the little wolf.

"C'mon, Angelita. Let's—" Sariel looked around

the sparsely appointed room, belatedly noticing there was nothing for the two of them to do but sit on the floor and wait. A level of hell where minutes passed like hours with no distractions. "Well...shit."

Angelita whined and bumped into her legs, offering comfort in her own way. Sariel sighed and dropped her hand to Angelita's neck to tug on the fur.

"He'll be okay. We'll all be okay."

The words tasted false on her lips. Would Bez be able to win a battle with the men who'd taken them? One-on-one, she believed Bez could do anything. Even two-on-one. But no man or wolf could take down a pack on their own, and if the men acted like a pack, Bez was in trouble. If the pack brought a werewolf, Bez was dead.

The silence reigned for several minutes, tension high, human and wolf breathing fast and hard as they waited for any sensory input that would tell them the fight had begun. Several minutes as Sariel's stomach churned and her heart raced, worry over her mate's safety taking over her thoughts.

The fight itself didn't start with a growl or a bang, not with anything loud or crashing. No, this fight started with a catcall from outside playing live over some kind of speaker system.

"Here, pretty girl. Come out and play with us." The words exploded into the room, shattering the silence. The voice came from a guard both women feared. His eyes were too wandering, his smile too lascivious. Sariel had hated him from the moment he'd looked her up and down when she'd been dropped at their houseboat camp. She hated him even more knowing his presence put Angelita and her mate in danger.

"Come on, girl," another wolf said from the opposite side of the house. "Your pack didn't hide when we came for them. They may not have been any good at fighting, but at least they died with some kind of honor instead of hiding away. Well, except your parents, of course."

Sariel grabbed Angelita as the shewolf growled, wrapping her arms around her fur-covered ribs and pulling her into a full-body hug. "They're trying to bait you so you react emotionally and make a mistake. Don't let them win."

Angelita growled and snapped, wiggling to break free. Sariel gripped her harder, wrapping her legs around Angelita's hips to hold her still.

"They all deserve to die for what they did to your pack. But you have to let Bez handle it, okay? He'll make sure they get what's coming to them."

Finally, Angelita huffed and held still, no longer fighting. Sariel ran her hands over the girl's fur, trying to keep her calm as more taunts came from outside. The men from the camp had arrived, surrounding the house, which meant Bez had to fight off three at once. Sariel wasn't sure even her strong, soldier mate was good enough for those odds. Especially if the werewolf showed up.

"What was it they called you, little girl?" a man called. Sariel stiffened as Angelita's head spun, staring hard at the door leading out of the room.

Sariel leaned down and hissed, "Don't—"

"Angelita, right? The pack's little angel come to save them all."

Angelita leaped from Sariel's hold and stormed to the door, her growl deep and threatening. Sariel landed against the metal wall, her head hitting hard. Stars exploded before her eyes. She rolled, shaking off the sick feeling in her stomach and gripping the back of her head. Shit, that smarted.

She crawled to her knees as the little wolf scratched at the door. "Angelita, no! Don't let them win."

"Guess you couldn't save them, after all," the man yelled with a sarcastic chuckle. "Especially not your own brother."

Angelita slammed into the steel door, jumping up on her hind legs and clawing at the handle until the lock disengaged. The little wolf pushed open the door and raced out into the attic like her tail was on fire. Sariel hurried to her feet, weaving as her head spun but still putting one foot in front of the other. Quickly.

Before the younger wolf could do much more than jump at the window in the dormer, Sariel caught up with her. She wrapped her arms around the wolf from behind and brought her face to her ear.

"They want you to come out there upset. We make mistakes when we're hurting, and they'll take advantage of those. Don't let them win with words, hon. Wait... watch. Let Bez do his thing."

Angelita fought to be free, clawing Sariel's arms and legs as she whipped her head back and forth to bite. Sariel held on, having battled young wolf shifters for far too many years not to know how to keep from being bitten.

"Soon, Angelita. Soon. Let's get back inside the safe room, though. Okay? Otherwise, Bez's going to be distracted by us, and that's the last thing he needs. He has to fight them. He has to win against them."

Angelita stilled, her growl turning to a whine. Until the catcalling started again.

"C'mon, Angelita. Come out here and let me see if your blood tastes as sweet as your mother's."

Oh, hell. There really was no coming back from that, and Sariel knew it. Knew it, and prepared for the firestorm.

Angelita twisted, biting down on Sariel's bare arm. The pain radiated to her fingers, forcing Sariel to release the wolf. Angelita headed straight for the small window overlooking the side of the cabin, looking ready to break right through the glass to get outside. Sariel grabbed her again, the two struggling, one holding on for dear life, and one dying to be released. Sariel stood as she got a solid hold on the wolf, Angelita a snapping, snarling mess in her arms. The man outside must have seen them through the dirty glass because he turned their way and grinned.

"There you are, young one. C'mon out and play with me. I promise not to make your punishment take as long as it did when I skinned your dad. You can come too, dud. We've got a hungry beast waiting for you."

Angelita snarled at the laughing man, but not for long. A high-pitched whistle interrupted her. Screaming through the night, the sound made both women stop and stare. A silver flash, a splash of red, and the man's head fell to the ground a second before his body collapsed.

Sariel dropped Angelita and collapsed against the window frame, fingers pressed to the cool glass.

"Bez."

Sixteen

Bez slipped through the shadows, staying deep inside the house to avoid the windows. A loudmouth shouted from outside, but Bez knew that idiot was just a ruse. A distraction meant to attract Angelita's attention with bullshit about her pack to make her react emotionally. They'd probably planned to separate the girl from him and Sariel and whisk her away. But Bez had her locked up, and he wouldn't let her go outside if she left the safe room. Plus he'd never been one to fall for attempts at distraction. If one man outside was yelling and causing a ruckus, somewhere in the silence the real threat was coming for Angelita and his mate.

His *mate*.

He could still smell Sariel on him and taste her on his lips, could still feel her warm body against his. Thoughts of her distracted him but only in the best way. The woman was a firecracker, gorgeous and stunning while simultaneously dangerous if in the wrong hands. Bez hoped his were the right hands, because once he got rid of the wolves prowling around the house outside and dealt with the werewolf he knew would be coming along, he was going to light her up and see what happened. That was his motivation. Not orders, not Blaze's approval, or Dire Wolf pride. He wanted his mate in his den and in his bed. Wanted her screaming his name as he teased her endlessly. The fuckers outside were just an obstacle in his way.

Shaking off the thoughts of his mate, Bez edged his way into the kitchen and toward the window. He flattened his body to the wall as he peered outside, keeping his wolf at the forefront of his mind, letting his animal senses take over. He smelled the interloper before his eyes found him, caught the shadow of the dark wolf standing at the edge of the lawn. His ears picked up the heavy breathing of the animal, the raspiness that came from running too hard too far for an out of shape shifter. Weak...the animal was weak and tired, an easy kill.

Bez felt his canines descend, the hard enamel pushing through his gums as his ears lengthened and lifted. He needed to stay in his human form to fight, but his wolf could not be caged. The two had worked together for centuries this way, fighting their best when they shared the body. Half human, half animal…all lethal.

The wolf outside rocked on his paws, ready and waiting for whatever signals his leader had taught him. Obviously following orders, he stared up at the house, almost salivating for his shot at Angelita and Sariel. Bez nearly growled, his lips curling back over his teeth in a show of dominance even though the weaker wolf couldn't see him. The fucker wouldn't get a chance to complete his mission.

Slow and silent, Bez climbed onto the counter and curved his body around the edge of the window. He kept his breathing steady as he inched the window up, giving himself a mere few inches of space to work. Not that he needed more than that. There was a reason he'd chosen the weapons he had.

Grabbing a chakram from his pocket, Bez angled his body back as he slid in front of the window. The metal ring glinted in the moonlight, edges sharper than a razor. Light and deadly in the right hands, and his were definitely the right hands. The wolf outside never even looked toward Bez's window, too intent on his quarry. His focus working in Bez's favor.

Bez took a deep breath and jackknifed up, fully in front of the window. The wolf's eyes darted to the glass, but it was too late for him. With a swing of his arm, Bez sent the chakram flying through the small gap between the sash and the frame, metal disk hitting the target in the throat a split second later. The wolf never made a sound, barely had time enough to realize Bez was even in the window. He simply fell to his side and bled all over the grass.

Two down at the houseboats, one down on the grass, two to go. And one less threat to his mate.

The soldier in Bez mentally kicked himself for that thought even as he crawled off the countertop and moved into the hall. His job, his mission, was to get the Omega out, to keep her safe, and to question the men who took her. Nothing in Blaze's orders mentioned Sariel as none of the intel had said she was in the camp, but she would've been seen as collateral damage in the effort to save the primary target. Sariel's death would have been accepted as necessary had he left her behind, but he couldn't have left her. Blaze and Dante would probably dismiss that factor. But to change the overall goal of the mission, to go from capture to kill, could be seen as something akin to mutiny.

And Bez didn't give a fuck.

At that moment, when the wolves were literally at the door and it was time to protect the Omega, his thoughts were on Sariel. On his mate. On his need to protect *her*, keep *her* safe, get *her* to his den and use his body and his skills to make sure no one came near. He'd never felt the strain of a mission more, the fear of failing so strongly. The werewolf would show up, angry and hungry and ready for blood. Female shifter blood. His mate's blood. A thought that made his own run cold.

It was time to fight.

The shifter on the other side of the house yelled something about the taste of Angelita's mother's blood, changing Bez's direction and plan. He'd been too far inside of his head considering the threat they were all under. The loud shifter may have been weak, his plan simple, but he could easily get the girls killed with his big mouth. Words had a way of crawling under skin and breaking down logic faster than anything else did. Angelita was too young not to care, and that put her in danger of falling for the bullshit.

Slipping across the tile floor, Bez crept to the back door. He let his senses flare, let them stretch and reach to cover the property. Still no sign of the werewolf, but he could sense two other wolves. Bez snuck out the back door and around the side of the house, clinging to the shadows of the overhang, hurrying toward the shifter with the big mouth. The one who thought a war was fought with words and yelling. Bez knew wars were fought many different ways, but he liked to battle silently, in the shadows and on the fringes. And he loved to surprise his enemy.

Pulling another chakram from his pocket, Bez blew out a breath and focused on the man by the front porch.

His eyes morphed to their wolflike slant, his pupils opening to let in more light. The night pulled back, the shadows replaced with brightness. Bez's wolf peered across the lawn, sizing up the threat, marking with deadly precision every soft spot of the other animal. Bez let his wolf inspect the target before he took a deep breath and shifted his human consciousness back to the forefront.

"There you are, young one," the man yelled. Bez's focus disappeared, slipping away into the night air. The girls had left the safe room. The danger of this fight had just ratcheted up ten notches in the blink of an eye. His wolf slammed forward, throwing his senses out harder, searching for every heartbeat, every sound as he prepared to fight in the only way he knew how. Violent and dirty.

"C'mon out and play with me. I promise not to make your punishment take as long as it did when I skinned your dad. You can come too, dud. We've got a hungry beast waiting for you."

Bez's fear for his mate turned to dread as the wind shifted. The stench of death and rot wafted from the lake itself, nearly buried under the calmer, cooler scent of the water. Not at all where Bez would have expected an enemy to come from. And that's when his stomach sank. Bez had misjudged the plan. The enemy shifters weren't spread out around the house to collect the women after they reacted to the loudmouth. They were directing the werewolf to its prey, into the house. To get around Bez's wolf senses, the werewolf had swum to the property and was now mere yards away. Practically knocking on the damned door. And his mate was no longer secured in the safe room.

Unable to delay for a moment longer, Bez shifted his weight and pulled his arm back. The chakram slipped out of his fingers as his arm rushed forward, spinning so fast it whistled through the air. Not quite the silent way he liked to operate, but Bez had to admit the single second of confusion on the man's face before the flying disc took off his head was satisfying in ways nothing else could be.

The moment the chakram sliced through flesh, Bez took off at a full run toward the front door.

Four down. One to go, if Harkens had been right about only five guards. Plus a werewolf hunting what had quickly become the most important thing in Bez's world.

Seventeen

Silence reigned as Sariel stood in the shadows with her hand over her mouth. That man—that man who'd taken her, yanked her away from her pack, and held her against her will—lay dead on the ground down below. She wanted to feel sadness, to feel sickened at such a blatant act of aggression by Bez. She knew she should be disgusted by her mate's actions, but she wasn't.

Bez wasn't the evil one in the situation, her captors were.

That disgusting man had helped to shatter her life, had completely decimated Angelita's family, and had tormented them both. In the end, his death at the hands of Bez could be seen as justice earned, so that's how Sariel chose to see it. At least, his death was quick. If the act had been left up to her, she might have made him suffer.

Angelita whined and wiggled in between her legs, forcing Sariel's thoughts away from the dead man on the grass. She followed as the red wolf crept closer to the window. Angelita hopped up on her rear legs, putting her front paws on the windowsill. The little wolf pressed her black nose to the glass, inspecting the scene below. For long, quiet moments, the wolf just stared at the body in the grass. Her wolf form quiet and still, barely breathing. But then she turned and gave Sariel a wide-eyed look of confusion.

Sariel blew out a breath and quickly got her words in order. Even in wolf form, Angelita looked so innocent, so young standing in the moonlight, staring up at her. But she wouldn't lie to the girl. Not after all they'd gone through together.

"He's dead." Sariel stroked Angelita's head and rubbed behind her ears. "We don't have to worry about him anymore. Bez took care of it."

Angelita huffed and looked back outside, brave in the face of such a horrific scene. Sariel felt so much maternal love for the young Omega, seeing a lot of what she wanted for herself in the girl. Angelita may have been small and young, but deep down, she was a warrior. And Sariel was going to make sure she was going to live to fight for a very, very long time.

Steps quiet but sure, Sariel moved to the window on the opposite side of the room. At first, the grassy lawn appeared quiet and empty, clear of attackers, but then she saw it. A dark lump lying on the lawn, rump brushing the tall grasses along the edge of the driveway. Two men dead, both at the hands of her mate.

Sariel almost felt guilty as a rush of pride washed over her. Bez was proving his strength and skill, even if doing so ended the life of other shifters. Pack justice could be harsh and cruel, but the punishment of death was a rarity, at least where she'd lived. Bez killing those men didn't thrill her, but she couldn't fault him for it. He was acting as a strong Alpha would—doing anything necessary to keep his pack safe. And at least on this horrible night, she and Angelita were his pack.

The longer the quiet of the night loomed dark and heavy, the more Sariel's nerves frayed. She kept waiting for a larger attack, for the sounds of fighting to reach her ears, but she heard nothing. Just the sounds of the night insects and animals going about their lives around them. Where were the other men from the camp? Bez had said there'd been three outside, which meant the fight was now one-on-one, and that was only if they hadn't brought the werewolf with them. As big and strong as Bez obviously was, she didn't like the thought of his being attacked by such a beast.

Needing to make sure her mate was okay, Sariel crept along the floor toward the access panel. She knew it was wrong, this decision, but she couldn't help herself. Like the clueless teenager in a campy horror movie, she moved toward the danger instead of away from it. If she could lift the ladder, she could crack the panel open, maybe look downstairs. The attic didn't allow a lot of scent input from the house, the ceiling under her feet too insulated or something. She needed a quick look and sniff, and then she'd take Angelita back into the safe room and lock the door.

Sariel had taken two steps when the sound of breaking glass shattered the silence. Soft, almost melodic, it splintered through the air, leaving behind a weighted anxiety in the quiet night. Her heart raced, the beat pounding in her ears as she waited for something more. For another sign of what was happening below their attic hiding spot.

For seconds that lasted far too long, Sariel stood on one foot, the other outstretched and ready to step, her toes pointed as they brushed the floor. Yet she didn't move, too afraid of setting the night off-balance with a noise. With a single squeak or bump.

Willing herself not to make a noise, Sariel shifted forward, placing her weight on the ball of her foot. Before she could drop her heel, a roar of fury and rage sounded that nearly shook the house to the foundation. Sariel screamed and jumped back, rushing toward Angelita as the crashes and growls of a true battle broke out downstairs. Walls shook, floors vibrated, and the grunts and snarls of shifters fighting to the death made her race across the wood floor. It wasn't the first time Sariel had heard the noise that came with a shifter fight, but it was the first time she'd had to worry about the safety of her mate while listening.

Eyeing the safe room door, she grabbed Angelita under the ribs and lifted her into her arms. To keep Bez focused, she'd make sure Angelita was in that safe room, no matter what. Bez's mission was to save the Omega, and damn it if she'd let her mate fail.

As the sounds grew closer, Sariel hoisted a fighting Angelita into the metal box. The little wolf twisted and turned, doing her best to escape. But Sariel wouldn't be deterred. She wrestled the canine form across the threshold and carefully tossed her toward the back of the room. Hurrying, she reached for the handle and yanked on the door, but before she could close it, the noises stopped. Not petered out, not moved away, just stopped, leaving her standing in a weighted silence once again. Her heavy breathing the only noise in the room.

Sariel's heart raced as her eyes locked on that attic access panel. As she waited for something from below. Some sign that her mate was still down there, still fighting.

Still alive.

Eighteen

The stench of death and rot increased as Bez turned the corner of the house. Pausing in the shadows of the porch, he pulled his wolf forward to give him a taste of the air. The animal inside shivered and growled, his hackles rising. That scent meant danger to the duo, it meant pain. The last time the two had hunted a werewolf without backup, they'd come out of the fight victorious...but not by much. They couldn't fail this time. There was something more important—more vital to Bez and his wolf—in that house. Something more important than the need to follow orders.

Bez stalked through the shadows, searching for signs of the werewolf. The beast had to have come in from the lake; it only made sense with the way his scent hid beneath by the smell of water. Creeping down the length of the house, Bez pushed his senses to the max. His head throbbed with the input—every sound of the forest, every lap of the lake—but he didn't let up. He pushed harder, maxing out his immense capabilities until he finally pinpointed something. A raspy intake of breath. Fifty yards down shore, hidden in the high grasses that surrounded most of the lake.

Bez focused on that spot and brought out more of his wolf. Ears lifting, muzzle extending, he crept around the house to the far side of the garage before dropping to the ground and crawling toward the shelter of the grass. This kill had to come fast and as a surprise. He could *not* let that werewolf anywhere near the girls.

It was time to hunt the hunter.

He slithered through the grass as silent as a snake. This moment, this hunt, was what he'd trained for all those years; this was what he knew. Get in, eliminate the target, get out. Something he'd done a thousand times, if not more. The fact that the target was a werewolf added a bit of risk but not enough to slow him down. He needed to eliminate the threat.

The werewolf crouched on the lakeshore. More humanoid than canine, but not really either in form, the creature stared at the house. His face was drawn and stretched, revealing a canine snout in the center of what should have been a human face. His body covered in a bristly fur, his human skin peeking through in patches and along joints. Legs bent and twisted somewhere between dog and not, hands tipped in dark, thick claws. A true monster.

As Bez slipped closer, keeping one hundred percent of his focus on the creature, the dread making his stomach churn grew. From where he lay and watched, it appeared as if the kidnappers had trained the beast somehow. The werewolf sat still, tense, and ready, every bit of his energy focused on the house. Bez could feel the anticipation pouring off the animal, the excitement. It certainly seemed to be waiting for some kind of order or direction. But werewolves weren't known for their trainability or intelligence once the animal took over the human. Unlike shifters, who had a constant stream of consciousness with their animal side, werewolves were human for so many days out of the month and beast the rest. There was no crossover, the human side sometimes even going back to work each day not knowing they'd turned into such a creature at night. But whatever this team had done, they'd done it well. The werewolf waited, drooling in what Bez assumed was hunger, twitching with his need for female flesh. Too bad he wouldn't be getting a taste.

Without a sound, Bez leaped out of the grass and onto the werewolf's back. The beast gave a surprised growl and jumped to its feet, swinging its arms in an attempt to dislodge the attacker. Bez held tight to his neck, his claw-tipped fingers puncturing the werewolf's thick flesh. Knees tight on his hips, hands gripping his throat, Bez kept a slow increase on his pressure, digging his claws deeper, forcing more and more blood from the beast's throat. Werewolves weren't like shifters, who died when their blood stopped flowing. No, werewolves could only be killed by a beheading. Without another chakram at his disposal, though, Bez had to improvise. So he gripped and squeezed and slowly cut his way through the thick, heavy flesh of the werewolf's neck. A gruesome way to kill, but effective.

The beast fought hard, dropping and rolling as it grunted, but Bez could not be deterred. If the werewolf lived, his mate could end up as the beast's target. And Bez wouldn't allow that. Not for a moment…not a single chance. The werewolf had to die, and Bez would accomplish that task by any means necessary.

The werewolf stumbled up the grass toward the house, obviously attempting to growl or yell, but Bez's hands constricted his airway too much for him to do much more than grunt. As the beast's air supply ran out and he weakened from the blood loss, the werewolf fell to his knees, taking Bez with him. Bez should have been ready, should have known the animal would give him one last fight, but he was too focused on increasing his grip and fighting his way through the thick, corded flesh with his claws.

As a last-ditch effort to unseat Bez, the werewolf flipped onto his back. He slammed his head into Bez's, making the shifter see stars. One second, that's all it took. The force of the blow caused Bez to release his grip just enough for the beast to let loose a throaty roar that actually shook the ground beneath Bez's back. There was no way any other shifters who'd come to take Angelita back hadn't heard the sound. Hell, there was probably no way the humans hadn't heard it if they were anywhere in the vicinity. Bez's cover had been blown; no more fighting in silence.

Snarling, refusing to surrender or risk his focus, Bez jumped up and regained his grip on the animal's throat. The two crashed through the grasses to the lawn, one bucking and swinging, the other clinging to the beast for all he was worth. It took longer than Bez would have liked, but finally, the werewolf fell to his knees once more. This time, Bez kept his hold strong but monitored the werewolf's actions carefully, watching for any signs of fight left in the beast. Lucky for him, there was none. Bez gripped tighter, sliding to the side as the werewolf fell onto its back, breathless and dazed, too tired to fight much more.

Bez used the position of the beast to his advantage, kneeling on its chest and placing one booted foot under its chin. Claws out and deep in the werewolf's flesh, Bez curled his fingers, grabbing hold of every bit of flesh in the werewolf's throat that he could, and yanked while kicking the werewolf's chin. The beast went still, his head rolling slightly to one side, no longer attached to its body. Bez gave himself a single moment, just long enough to take three greedy, deep pulls of air, before he stumbled toward the house.

His stomach sank and his legs pushed harder as he approached. The back door had been left open, the glass shattered. A sure sign the enemy had gotten inside. And he had no idea if his mate was back in the safe room or not.

Four down, werewolf defeated, one to go. He hoped.

Nineteen

Seconds stretched into minutes as Sariel stood in the open safe room door, the silence bearing down on her like a weight. Not a sound, not a sense; the entire house sat still and empty. The level of quiet disconcerted her, made her practically taste it. Not a single noise from nature broke the oppressive night, no bug or animal or wind rattling trees. The world had stopped, and with it so had Sariel's heart. In theory.

Angelita brushed against Sariel's leg, her fur a familiar touch that still made Sariel shudder. The two inched forward, eyes trained on the access panel to the floor below. A scent crept through the heavy night air, one of rot, of swamp. Putrid and wet, the scent grew stronger, creeping into their silent little world. Angelita growled low and soft, barely above a whisper. Sariel glanced down at the wolf, silencing her with a look before taking another step forward.

Two more steps across the rough wood floor, and Sariel paused. Listening. Opening her senses to what disturbed the still night air. Something scratched at the ceiling below them, a soft, rough sound that kick-started Sariel's heart and threw it into overdrive.

"Bez?" she whispered, taking one more slow step. A few more inches gained. And she took a breath.

The access panel exploded into the attic, shards of wood and pieces of the drywall flying through the air. Sariel screamed as Angelita barked, both falling backward to the floor. A man from the camp, one of their kidnappers, jumped through the hole in the floor, landing on the balls of his feet only a few yards in front of Sariel.

"I've been looking for you," he growled, his eyes locked on Angelita's wolf form.

"Go," Sariel yelled, shoving the animal toward the safe room as she hurried to her feet. She planted herself between Angelita and the angry shifter, feet wide, hands up and ready to fight. "You can keep right on looking because you don't get to take her again."

"Oh, really?" he asked, snorting a laugh. "How exactly do you intend to stop me? I've taken care of your little guard dog downstairs."

Sariel's heart shattered, bursting into flames that sent her reeling, leaving nothing behind but scarred walls and a sooty mess on her soul. Her mate…he had to be talking about her mate. Her Bez.

But as the man took a step in her direction, Sariel pushed aside the fire burning her alive from the inside out. She'd deal with the loss of her mate later. If Bez was dead, he died battling to save Angelita. Those were his orders, and Sariel wouldn't let him fail. With a power she'd never drawn on before buzzing under her skin, she gave herself over to her wolf, letting the beast within have control even as she stayed in her human form.

"You may have gotten past him, but you won't get through me. Not tonight." Sariel snarled and ducked low, ready to battle. But just before she leaped, a muscled arm reached through the hole in the floor and gripped the man's ankle, yanking him backward and forcing him to fall through the floor to the lower level. Sariel froze, not sure she'd seen what she thought she had. Not knowing if she could believe the sight of that hand she recognized. Big and thick, that hand looked just like one that had grabbed her hip, had slid up her thigh, had made her wet with its blunt fingers and rough skin.

She *knew* that hand.

At the sound of a vicious snarl from below, Sariel rushed to the edge of the hole in the floor, the scene below making her breath catch. Bez, half-naked and bloodied, had the kidnapper in a kind of headlock, one the man was desperately trying to escape. His flailing and jerking were hindered by blood on the wood floor, though. His own, she hoped.

As the kidnapper continued to struggle, Sariel leaned out farther, her hand catching her weight on the opposite side of the hole. The buzz inside grew stronger, more vibrant, becoming a physical link she felt to her mate. She'd heard the stories of the Omega strength, of the power they brought to their packs, but she'd never felt it for herself. That buzz, that power, was undoubtedly coming from her wolf, and she felt the energy flow from her to her mate. Backing up Bez, even though she didn't know how it was happening.

Bez growled and yanked, eyes meeting hers for a single, tense moment, before finally stabilizing his footing and jerking his arm around the other man's neck. His clawlike fingers cut through the flesh, tips stained red with blood. A fast death for a bad man, brought about by a skilled warrior. Strong, efficient, and effective.

Bez dropped the man's body to the floor and looked up, chest heaving as he met Sariel's gaze. God, he looked so wild, so completely animal even in his human form. A true wolf in a man's body. The two shared a moment filled with fire and passion, with desire and need. A moment of shared power and relief. Of connection.

"You good?" Bez asked, his voice rough like sandpaper against her ears. Sariel nodded, unable to speak. Too damned relieved to worry about silly things like words.

Bez held out a hand, keeping his eyes on hers. "Get down here, Freckles."

Sariel shivered at the command in his voice. Without pause, she dropped through the ceiling, landing with a soft thud as Bez guided her. Before he could speak, she reached up and wrapped her arms around his neck, pressing her lips to his. She poured every emotion she felt into that kiss—fear, anxiety, relief, and even lust. As much as Sariel should have been scared by all the death around her, she couldn't be. Seeing her mate so strong and capable, as a victorious protector, was one of the biggest turn-ons she'd ever experienced. She wanted to make sure he knew that.

Bez returned her kiss with equal fervor, running his hands over her hips to grasp her ass and yanking her off her feet. She wrapped her legs around his waist, holding him tight to her body, rubbing against where he was quickly becoming hard for her. She wished for nothing to be in between them. For flesh on flesh, hard on soft, knowing the slightest shift on either's part would take them from third base to a home run. Craved it. Needed to know that if she just angled her hips like—

A soft bark from above broke the spell woven between the two. Bez jerked and spun Sariel against the wall, caging her in with his body. Protecting her as always. Sariel growled, her tongue licking her bottom lip to savor her mate's taste. She stared at Bez's mouth, desperate for more of his touch, needing him in ways that defied the reality around them. But at least he seemed to feel the same. He growled low, his hands squeezing her ass harder, pulling her closer. Offering her one final tease before he glanced at Angelita overhead.

"Still a wolf, huh?" Bez ran his nose along Sariel's cheek, a deep chuckle rumbling through his chest. "Let's get you down."

Bez carefully unwound Sariel's legs from his hips. As her feet touched the floor, she ran her nose along Bez's breastbone and clutched at his arms. Trembling. Never wanting to let go.

"You made it safe for her," Sariel whispered. She pulled back, staring up at him with pride.

Bez's ice-blue eyes met hers, filled with a thousand untold emotions. "For you. I made it safe for you."

Twenty

The roar of incoming vehicles met Bez's ears barely an hour after the fight ended. He looked up from his spot on the front porch, gripping Sariel tighter. They'd each gotten dressed in the sweat pants and T-shirts Bez had found in one of the closets inside the house before making their way to the porch, neither wanting to go back inside with the body and the bloodstained floors. Bez sat with his back against the wall and Sariel curled in his lap, her head resting on his chest. Angelita lay beside them with her head on his knee and her paw on Sariel's hand. The three cuddled together in what reminded Bez of a puppy pile, all touching, all warm and safe.

And he had to admit, he liked it.

Angelita heard the approaching fleet a few

moments after Bez, her ears pricking. She whined as the sound grew louder, the air practically vibrating with the rumble of large combustion engines.

"We're good, little one," Bez said, smoothing his hand over her head. "It's my pack."

Sariel didn't respond, just pressed herself against Bez's chest and held tight to his arms. Something he found to his liking. Bez's Dire brothers turned onto the driveway mere moments later. Two rode in on motorcycles, the third bringing up the rear in a behemoth of a Suburban. The truck's windows shook with the percussive sound of the hard rock the driver was blasting, making Bez's ears hurt. Still, he'd never been so grateful to see them.

"Stay here," he whispered to Sariel as he glanced at Angelita. "You, too."

With one final stroke of his mate's arm, Bez lifted her and placed her next to Angelita, letting them form their own pile while he stood up and strode off the porch. Chin up, chest out, ready to defend his actions, Bez approached his brethren. Mammon was the first off his bike.

"What's up, Bez? We hunting tonight?"

"Negative." Bez gave the man a big, back-slapping hug. "All targets have been eliminated."

Levi hopped out of the truck, meeting Bez for another rough greeting. "I thought the mission was retrieval, not elimination."

"It was." Bez waited for Thaus to stroll over from his bike. Bigger than the other Dires, the man exuded a sense of malice that most people found off-putting. It had never bothered Bez in the past, but knowing his mate was close by made him reevaluate. Thaus would probably terrify Sariel. He would definitely scare the little wolf. Something Bez found objectionable.

Bez looked each man in the eye as they formed a small circle. "The mission changed when I found the camp. There were two Omegas, not one."

"Standard collateral issue during retrieval," Thaus murmured, his disapproval clear. "Acquire the target as ordered and reconvene at a later time to strategize for the second retrieval."

Bez shook his head. "I couldn't leave her behind. She's an Omega."

"We would have gone back for her," Thaus replied. "Taking her when you were unprepared endangered the life of the target. You should have left the extra until we could assemble a proper team."

"She's not just an extra. I couldn't leave her because she's—" Bez paused, the words harder to say than he could have guessed "—she's my mate."

The three Dires didn't respond, didn't move or even blink as they stared at him. Bez didn't flinch under their scrutiny. He'd been ready for them to doubt him—their history definitely indicated they would never find mates. Hell, they probably thought he'd lost his mind.

"Not possible," Thaus grunted.

"Truth." Bez growled in warning, letting his wolf come to the surface. He knew they'd have to see the truth if his wolf claimed her; he just hoped they would believe the man first. "I found my mate, and there was no fucking way I was leaving her in that camp with those men. The bastards were going to use her as werewolf bait. There was no time. I made the call based on the situation I was in, and I'd do it again."

Levi shook his head. "Blaze is going to—"

"Blaze will just have to accept my actions."

Levi's eyes went wide, his surprise evident. Bez had never gone against Blaze. Not once in all their years working for him. For him to be willing to risk Blaze's ire certainly seemed to indicate the gravity of the situation in which Bez found himself.

"Show me," Thaus said, still not sounding as if he even believed in the possibility of a Dire mating.

Bez nodded and turned back toward the porch. His wolf paced in his mind, angry that his brothers didn't believe him, but Bez wasn't ready to give up the hope that they would. They'd lived far too long mateless to be willing to accept this new bond without reservation. Bez understood that. Didn't make it any easier, though, to be doubted by his pack.

Bez rushed up the stairs to a very curious Sariel. "Come."

He held out his hand, furrowing his brow when

anger flashed in her eyes. Angelita growled softly, a warning sound. One he understood and took to heart.

"Please, Freckles. Come with me?"

Sariel paused, looking past him to where the other Dires stood before placing her little hand in his. That moment, the amount of trust she gave him, was enough to soften the fury boiling up inside. Enough to shove all the worry to the back of his mind. They'd deal with his pack together.

Bez led her to where his brothers stood, keeping her tucked into his side. She trembled as she walked, though she never tried to stop him, allowing him to lead her where he wanted to go. Another sign of trust he appreciated. Angelita trailed after them, refusing to be left behind.

"Brothers, this is Omega Sariel. She's my mate." Bez stood with Sariel by his side, staring each man down in turn. This was his mate, his fated match, and no one would refuse him his right to call her that so long as she allowed it.

Silence stretched between the groups, tense and dark. Bez's wolf surged forward, ready for a fight. Bez knew the guys would sense the shift, feel the power of his wolf. Hell, they'd see it in the swirl of his blue eyes. His wolf would stake their claim for them if he had to; he'd also fight one of his own brothers for his mate. No one would be keeping Sariel and him apart.

Finally, after far longer than Bez was happy to wait,

Thaus huffed.

"One of our own, come home to us at last." He leaned down to Sariel's height and gave her his best interpretation of a grin. "Blessings to you, Omega, and welcome to our Dire Wolf pack."

"Hey," Levi called, giving Sariel a fake pout. "Don't we get a chance to meet our little sister? Or are you going to hide behind the big lug here forever?"

Bez laughed and urged Sariel to take a step in front of him, keeping his arms wrapped around her shoulders. "Sariel, this is Mammon, Levi, and Thaus. Three of my Dire Wolf brothers."

"Uh...hi." Sariel waved, clinging to Bez's arm with her other hand. He hated that the guys frightened her, but he knew she'd learn to trust them all. She was pack now, and Dires would fight to the death for their pack.

As Bez cuddled Sariel closer, wanting to offer his body as protection from the other Dires she saw as a bit of a threat, Thaus smirked.

"Blaze is still going to have your pelt."

Twenty-one

I have to commend you, Bez," Dante said as he looked over the little cabin by the lake. "You really pulled this one off, even with the added challenges the job presented."

Bez pursed his lips. "Challenges, sir?"

"Well, meeting your mate can be rather distracting. I should know; I've been through it twice." He glanced over his shoulder to where Blaze and Moira stood. The curvy shewolf leaned against the side of the helicopter that would be taking her and her mates back to the airport with Angelita. Blaze, on the other hand, paced and yelled into his phone, obviously upset. Most likely about Bez killing off the kidnappers. Something Bez was still waiting to hear about from the leader of the NALB.

"I have no idea how you managed to keep the Omega safe when your mate was threatened," Dante said, drawing Bez's attention back to him. "I don't think I could have done it."

Before Bez could answer, Sariel herself walked up, sliding her arm around Bez's waist. "He was very calm and focused. There was no way he could have failed."

"Of course not. Bez never fails." Dante smiled, turning to Bez's mate. "I'm quite happy to meet you, Omega Sariel. I have to admit, your story has taken me a bit by surprise. An Omega we knew nothing about and a Dire Wolf with a mate, who would have thought?"

"Not me, sir." Bez grinned as Sariel smacked him in the chest.

"She's got your number, Bez. I'd be careful with your words." Dante glanced between the two, grin firmly in place. "I'm thrilled he found you, Sariel. Bez here needs a good strong woman by his side."

Sariel grinned. "As do most men."

Bez rolled his eyes at Dante's laugh, and he hugged his mate closer to feel her giggle. "Are you heading right back to Chicago?"

"Yes, Moira and I want to update the Feral Breed specialists on this incident as soon as we can convene the team. We'll need them to help us find this north camp." He raised an eyebrow at the two of them. "Especially with our most successful hunter out for a few weeks."

"Out?" Sariel asked, looking up at Bez with wide eyes. He glared at Dante, having not had the time to tell her the news yet.

"Bez has a mate now," Dante said with a smile. "I think he'd like to take a little time to settle in to your relationship. Blaze and I did the same after Moira joined our triad. It made the transition for her much easier. Besides, our boy here deserves a break."

"Our boy deserves a disciplinary hearing," Blaze said, storming over. Anger poured off him, from the stiff set of his shoulders to the hard glare on his face.

"Blaze," Dante started, but his mate wouldn't let him finish. Blaze stalked right up to Bez, nearly bumping into Sariel. Bez growled and pulled his mate to the side, moving her out of the way as much as possible while keeping a hand on her arm.

"You were to retrieve the kidnappers, not eliminate them."

Bez growled, refusing to back down. "They were a threat to two Omegas."

"They were the key to finding the others, and you slaughtered them without permission. There had to have been another way."

Levi appeared almost out of nowhere, sliding into a spot on Bez's flank. "Are you doubting the word of a Dire Wolf, sir?"

Blaze took a step back from the pair, growling. "None of you has ever given me reason to before today."

Before Bez could react, Thaus stepped between him and Bez, flanked by Mammon. A wall of Dire muscle blocking Bez from the person they saw as a threat, tucking Sariel behind them as well. Something Bez noted with appreciation.

"Our allegiance—while graciously shared with you, Blaze—is primarily for our pack," Thaus said, glaring at the NALB president. "Sariel is an Omega, of the lineage of the Dires. She is from the blood of our pack and, therefore, under our protection. Dire Beelzebub was acting with the full support of all the Dire Wolves in retrieving and protecting her."

Blaze and Thaus stared one another down, neither willing to lose the challenge the other threw. Bez stood at his brother's shoulder, ready to jump in and defend his actions again. For all the years he'd worked with Blaze, he'd never seen the man so wound up, so angry. But Bez refused to apologize—his mate had been in danger. A fact that justified his actions...period.

Finally, Blaze huffed, glancing from one Dire shifter to the next. "All the Omegas are in danger."

"And we'll do our absolute best to protect them," Thaus said, moving to stand beside Sariel. "Every last one of them."

"You'd better." Blaze shook his head, his anger deflating a bit. "I apologize, Sariel. I'm concerned for your Omega sisters."

"As am I, President Blasius." Sariel stood her ground, head up, staring hard at the powerful shifter. Bez practically burned with pride for his mate, whose bravery continued to impress him.

Blaze smiled, the tension in the air drifting away as he shook his head. "Please, call me Blaze."

Angelita padded up cautiously, staying close to Sariel as she regarded the new shifters on the property. Bez and his three Dire Wolf brothers had been joined by eight members from the nearest Feral Breed denhouse, all ready to protect the young Omega. The reactions from the men ranged from relief to disappointment when they realized Bez had already exterminated the targets plus a werewolf. His own pack more disappointed than the others. Especially Levi, who had a slight werewolf obsession.

"Bez, great job on this mission," Blaze said. Bez knew that was about as much of an apology as he'd get, not that the words mattered. As long as his mate and their bond were respected, he'd continue fighting to keep the Omegas safe. All of the Omegas.

"Thank you, sir."

"And congratulations on your mating. Please, take some time to settle in to your new life. We need more Dire Wolves in the world." Blaze smiled and glanced back at the chopper, but Bez focused on Sariel. Her face had fallen, her eyes dropping to the red wolf leaning into her leg. She couldn't have children, which meant no new Dires. Bez was fine with that, was happy to share his life with only her, but by the look in her eyes, Sariel might want more. And the more at this point was Angelita.

"More Dires?" Levi asked, chuckling. "Shit, that's all we need. Tiny terrors running all over the place and terrorizing all the supernaturals."

Thaus snorted a laugh. "That'd only be yours, Levi."

"Mine? Hell no. Never going to happen." Levi shook his head, firm in his denial.

Blaze laughed. "Now you've done it."

Levi's brow drew down in confusion. "Done what?"

"Tempted the fates. Expect to be mated next, young Leviathan." Blaze grinned and raised his eyebrows almost in a challenge. "I look forward to seeing the type of woman strong enough to tame the likes of you."

Levi huffed, looking irritated. "With all due respect, sir—you're crazy. Bez here is the first Dire to find his mate in centuries. I don't see anyone of the rest of us pairing up anytime soon."

Blaze just grinned. "We shall see, boy. We shall see."

With a single lift of Blaze's arm, the blades on the helicopter began to spin, indicating it was time for them to leave.

Dante smiled down at the little wolf who was still wrapped around Sariel's leg. "Well, young one. Looks like it's our time to go."

Angelita whined and crept back, almost hiding

behind Bez's mate. Bez growled on instinct, the fear in his charge something he didn't like. He almost wanted to tell the men no, that Angelita would be coming with him and Sariel. But, not for the first time, his mate beat him to it.

Sariel dropped to her knees and pulled the wolf into her arms. "You call me when they're done pumping you for information, ya hear? I'll come running."

"*We'll* come running." Bez offered the wolf a pat on the head. He brought his gaze up to a furious-looking Blaze. "Angelita is part of our pack now, part of the Dire legend. Once the brass is finished, she'll be coming home to live with Sariel and me."

"Bez," Dante said, a warning in his voice.

"She's old enough to decide for herself." Sariel stood tall, her voice forceful even in the face of such powerful shifters. A perfect example of the strength and bravery of the Omegas. "What do you say, Angelita? Want us to come get you from Chicago in a few weeks?"

The young wolf barked and weaved herself between the legs of Bez and Sariel, making her preference known.

Bez raised an eyebrow at Blaze. "Decision's made. Sariel and I will see you in three weeks to pick up Angelita."

"I can bring her back," Levi said, dropping down to wrap an arm around the wolf. Staking his claim for his pack in every motion. "I'm heading up to Chicago to meet with Shadow from the Feral Breed. I'll bring her to you when I'm finished."

"Even better." Bez patted Angelita on the head. "You're safe with my brother. He'll look out for you, okay? And you keep trying to come back to your human side while you're there. It's hard but worth it."

The little wolf huffed but headed for the helicopter, her tail tucked low and her head down. Bez felt an odd pang in his heart watching Angelita walk off, knowing how much the girl meant to his mate...and to him. The little wolf walked slowly across the grass, obviously scared. But she'd be back soon, and she and Sariel would become his responsibility. One he took on with a sense of honor and pride.

The Dire Wolves stood together, watching the shifters head for the chopper. Mammon, Levi, and Thaus... His brothers, his pack. They formed a subtle V, keeping Sariel between them, guarding the new shewolf added to their ranks. And though Bez had no idea how her presence would go over with the entire team, he knew they would all protect her. She was an Omega, one of their own, their bonds hidden for centuries, the women practically lost in plain sight.

And so was Angelita.

Without thought to what he was doing, Bez stepped forward and whistled. Blaze, Dante, and Angelita all turned as they reached the chopper, joining Moira in looking over the Dire pack.

"Your pack deserves justice, Angelita. And we're going to get that for you." Bez glanced at his teammates, knowing they'd all follow his lead if he set the mandate. "We'll track them all. Every shifter or werewolf who took part in the murder of your kin. We'll track them, and we'll catch them. And when we do, we'll eliminate the threat they pose. You will never be harmed again. On our honor."

The other Dire men repeated the vow, heads up and voices strong. Bez knew the challenge he'd laid down, knew the difficulties and danger that would come from it, but he wouldn't let the girl down. He'd never fail an Omega again, and his team wouldn't fail him.

Readers who purchased the electronic version of SAVAGE SURRENDER are able to access to a bonus scene through the author's newsletter. All print buyers have automatic access to this scene. Enjoy!

The Jeep rolled into a small town late in the afternoon, just as the sun was falling toward the flat Texas horizon. The whole place could be missed if you blinked, almost literally. A gas station, a minimart kind of grocery store, a tiny hardware-slash-general store, and a whole slew of empty storefronts decorated the main street. The houses and farms sat farther out with acres and acres of land separating them. The entire area was sparse but beautiful in a rugged sort of way. The land reminding Sariel of the man at her side.

She had readily jumped at the chance to leave the swamp behind when Bez asked her to go with him. Well, not asked. He told her they'd be going to Texas for a while, to hole up in case anyone else came looking for her. But she was okay with being told what to do *that* time… The man was trying to protect his mate. If he felt his ranch in Texas was the best place for that, so be it.

"It's…nice," Sariel said, breaking the silence they'd been riding in for the past few hours. "Different from where I grew up."

Bez grunted and kept driving, passing wire fences separating the road from the cows that roamed the flat ground and the farm fields green and ripe with whatever was growing. He drove for another ten minutes down unmarked dirt roads before slowing the Jeep. Out to where town was a memory, where fields and pastures met the horizon. Bez turned onto a dirt path that had probably once been a driveway of sorts, taking them through a small grove of trees. The rutted, almost abandoned path curved one final time to reveal the prettiest low-slung log home Sariel had ever seen. Wide and sprawling with a deep front porch that spanned the length, the house screamed of home, comfort, and family, even though she could tell no one had lived in it for a number of years.

Bez stopped in front of the house and turned off the engine. The sounds of birds and insects chattering filled the air, making Sariel smile. She turned to ask him about the house, but the words died on her tongue. He stared past her, his eyes almost glowing, his jaw hard and his shoulders stiff. She stared right back, waiting him out, somehow knowing whatever it was that had him on edge was important to him. To them.

"This is my home," he finally said, his voice rough and his words cautious. Sariel waited for more, watching him, observing and learning. The intensity in his gaze, the clenching of his jaw; he seemed almost ready for a fight. Perhaps preparing himself for a battle or...

Oh.

Sariel reached for his hand, running her fingers along the back.

"It's a real pretty house," she whispered once he finally met her gaze. He didn't respond at first, but she expected that, having finally figured something out about him. This stiff, silent act was Bez nervous. Afraid Sariel wouldn't like this place. The man who was more wolf than not was worried his den wouldn't be good enough for his mate. Silly wolf.

"We should... I want..." He trailed off, pursing his lips and clenching his hand into a fist under hers. "Can I show you?"

Sariel nodded, not quite sure what he meant but always willing to follow him. She stepped out of the truck and onto the dusty ground, staring at the house that obviously meant so much to her mate. The charm, how well it had been built, the little touches that showed the attention to detail. Hand-carved porch rails and rough-scraped wood planks, windows set deep within the walls and huge, heavy doors leading inside. All gorgeous. All appearing to be made by hand.

"You built this place, didn't you?"

Bez paused for only a moment before nodding. No words spoken, and yet none necessary. This was his home, one he built with his own two hands. This house was *him*.

He led the way to the front door, the steps creaking under their feet. Sariel sniffed, acclimating herself to the Texas wildlife and double-checking for the scents of other predators. Not that Bez hadn't already done that. There was no way he'd lead her into danger.

Bez held the door open, ducking his head as she passed, a low growl rumbling through him. Oh, yes, Sariel being in this place had her mate all tied up inside. Had his wolf showing his presence along with the man. She'd need to work extra hard to untangle the two. And she looked forward to it.

The large family-style room she walked into was devoid of furniture, but it had a huge fireplace along one wall and a fabulous view of the Texas landscape at the back. A kitchen, what looked like a dining room, wide-open halls leading off each side, and a door to what Sariel had to assume was a bathroom completed the first floor. Rustic and classic, charming and simple, the home sat as a perfect example of Bez's style.

"I love it." She smiled at Bez, who had his back to the door. Watching her. Always watching her.

"Good."

"Just good?" Sariel cocked her head, willing him to come to her, wanting to feel his hands on her body in the worst way.

But Bez didn't make a move. He simply nodded once and said, "We'll live here."

"That's it?" Sariel's heart hurt just a little at how casual he seemed. She knew he was a man of few words, but this was a big deal. They weren't just going to stay here for a few weeks and move on. She knew by the way his shoulders sat rigid and stiff, how his hand clung to the doorknob—he wanted them to live here permanently. This was his way of asking for a life together. But, again, not asking. Telling her.

"That's all you have to say?" Sariel huffed and shook her head. "You don't even ask; you just tell me to live here. You expect forever with me to be spent in this home, yet you say nothing but the bare minimum. That's not romantic, Bez."

Bez frowned as he finally stepped closer, pulling her into his arms. "If you wanted sweet words, you got the wrong mate."

"Obviously," she huffed.

He leaned down and nipped Sariel's lower lip, making her gasp. "I don't talk; I do. I'm direct and like directness back. If you don't want to live here, tell me now. But that's what I want."

Sariel stared at his chest, unable to look him in the eye. "And what if I *don't* want to live here? Where will you leave me?"

"Freckles," he whispered. She swallowed hard and looked up, almost afraid of what she'd see. But he stared down with a face full of emotion, his eyes soft and his lips curling into a smile. "I have a barn full of things to offer you—furniture and paintings, jewelry and baubles from around the world. Trinkets and shit that most humans covet; things I've collected as I've waited for you. All here on this land I've owned for decades. But if you don't like it, if you have no interest in this place, I'll get rid of it all. We'll go someplace else and start new."

"But you want to stay here?"

The twitch at the corner of his eye was his only tell. "I do... So long as it's with you."

Sariel's heart nearly exploded. For a man who used his words sparingly, he'd just said a lot, both in words and meaning. He wanted her to be with him. And she wanted to be wherever he was.

"Here." Sariel grinned, clinging to his shoulders. "I want to stay here with you if you'll have me."

"I'll always have you."

She leaned into his hold, rising up on the balls of her feet to reach his chin. "You sure about that?"

He growled as she nipped his chin, his fingers holding her hips with a hard grip. "Yes."

"What if we don't fit?" she asked, raising an eyebrow. "We've barely begun, really. What if other aspects of our relationship don't work out?"

"Like what?"

"Sex."

Bez pressed his hard length against Sariel's hip, grinding into her, showing her exactly how much his body wanted hers. "Not fucking possible."

"I don't know." She shook her head and gave him a very serious look. "That one time may have been a fluke. We might have bad sex together."

Bez reared back, obviously shocked. Sariel smiled and ran her hands over his chest to his hips, loving the feel of him under her palms.

"We should try it again," she said, dropping her voice and practically purring. "Before we make any big decisions, I mean."

"Try what?" Bez asked, his brow furrowed.

Sariel licked her lip and grinned. "Sex, of course."

Bez's surprised face turned to one of desire as he nodded. "Yes, we probably should. No one shoots a perfect target every time."

"Your shot, then," she said, voice deep with her own growl.

Without preamble, he spun them both and trapped her between him and the wall. "Gotcha."

"Yeah, you do."

Gentler than she expected, he leaned down and kissed her, his lips soft against hers. A lovely kiss filled with emotions and desire. A kiss of someone who showed his care with actions, not words. A kiss of a man learning what it meant to be kissed.

As Bez growled and slid his tongue against hers, he grabbed her hips and picked her up. Sariel wrapped her legs around his waist, remembering how they'd been in this exact same position mere hours ago, though with fewer clothes in the way. That time they'd been interrupted by Angelita, but there were no people here, no interruptions. It was just Bez and Sariel…and a desperate need to have her mate.

"I'm going to claim you," Bez whispered against her jaw, voicing the thoughts she'd been pondering. "If you don't want that, tell me now. Otherwise, I'm going to fuck you right here on this floor and give you my claiming bite."

Sariel wiggled in his hold until she had him lined up just right, a couple of layers of fabric and one push away from what they both wanted so badly. And then she brought her mouth to his ear and licked the shell of it.

"Make me yours, soldier."

And he did…multiple times and in every room of that cabin as well as the front porch. But that was okay, it was their house and they could do what they wanted, where they wanted. And they did for the weeks he stayed home with her, though they had to be a bit more subtle once Angelita rejoined them. But phone calls and missions rolled in eventually, as they'd known they would, each taking him away from her for days or weeks at a time.

Still, that little cabin in Texas was their home, the place they would always come back to. It morphed from a secret hiding place to the home base of the Dire Wolf pack, each male coming to stay with them and get to know their newest member. Sariel felt blessed by them, quickly befriending each one. She welcomed them into their space and showed them what family was like, what pack was for, and gave them a place to call home.

A place they all belonged...together.

Also from international bestselling author
Ellis Leigh

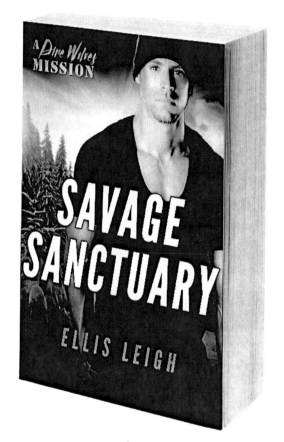

A *Dire Wolves* MISSION

Also
Available

FERAL BREED MOTORCYCLE CLUB
Claiming His Fate
Claiming His Need
Claiming His Witch
Claiming His Beauty
Claiming His Fire
Claiming His Desire

FERAL BREED FOLLOWINGS
Claiming His Chance
Claiming His Prize
Claiming His Grace

THE GATHERING
Killian & Lyra
Gideon & Kalie
Blasius, Dante, & Moira
Blasius, Dante, & Moira: Homecoming

About
the Author

A storyteller from the time she could talk, Ellis grew
up among family legends of hauntings, psychics, and
love spanning decades. Those stories didn't always
have the happiest of endings, so they inspired her
to write about real life, real love, and the difficulties
therein. From farmers to werewolves, store clerks to
witches—if there's love to be found, she'll write about
it. Ellis lives in the Chicago area with her husband,
daughters, and to tiny fish that take up way too much
of her time.

www.ellisleigh.com

CPSIA information can be obtained at www.ICGtesting.com
Printed in the USA
LVOW11s2151050516

486935LV00001B/1/P